I0543685

A COLLECTION OF
ROMANTIC SHORT STORIES

JEN TALTY

JUPITER PRESS

Deadly Secrets is the best of romance and suspense in one hot read!" *NYT Bestselling Author Jennifer Probst*

"A charming setting and a steamy couple heat up the pages in a suspenseful story I couldn't put down!" *NY Times and USA today Bestselling Author Donna Grant*

"Jen Talty's books will grab your attention and pull you into a world of relatable characters, strong personalities, humor, and believable storylines. You'll laugh, you'll cry, and you'll rush to get the next book she releases!" Natalie Ann USA Today Bestselling Author

"I positively loved *In Two Weeks*, and highly recommend it. The writing is wonderful, the story is fantastic, and the characters will keep you coming back for more. I can't wait to get my hands on future installments of the NYS Troopers series." *Long and Short Reviews*

"*In Two Weeks* hooks the reader from page one. This is a fast paced story where the development of the romance grabs you emotionally and the suspense keeps you sitting on the edge of your chair. Great characters, great writing, and a believable plot that can be a warning to all of us." *Desiree Holt, USA Today Bestseller*

"*Dark Water* delivers an engaging portrait of wounded hearts as the memorable characters take you on a healing journey of love. A mysterious death brings danger and intrigue into the drama, while sultry passions brew into a believable plot that melts the reader's heart. Jen Talty pens an entertaining romance that grips the heart as the colorful and dangerous story unfolds into a chilling ending." *Night Owl Reviews*

"This is not the typical love story, nor is it the typical mystery. The characters are well rounded and interesting." *You Gotta Read Reviews*

SOMEDAY MY RANGER WILL COME BY JEN TALTY

SOME DAY MY RANGER WILL COME

A Romantic Short Story
A 1001 Dark Nights Story Challenge Finalist

By
USA Today Bestselling Author
JEN TALTY

*E*lla Kane thought she knew her way around a motorboat, but she'd never actually had to captain one herself. Of course, when she went out on the Intracoastal, it wasn't in a fourteen-foot bathtub with an outboard engine that she controlled by holding a handle attached to it and not a steering wheel.

The guide at the dock told her that all she had to do was head south, stay in the main river, and she'd easily find Black Park Island and the campgrounds. She'd been on the water for almost an hour. She thought for sure she should have seen the park and its sexy ranger by now.

Thick, tropical trees spread their branches with lush green leaves over the water, making a canopy. And all she could think about was a snake dropping down on her head, or an alligator finding its way into her boat.

Birds dove down to the water, and fish flipped, splashing about, making her jump. She liked being outside and getting fresh air, but no one would ever call her the adventurous type.

The things she was willing to do to impress a man.

And not just any man.

Philip Prince was her knight in shining armor. Her one and only. Her diamond in the rough. If he were a frog and she kissed him, he'd likely turn into a prince. Now, all she had to do was show him that she wasn't the same self-absorbed girl she used to be without making too much of an ass of herself. And, in the process, bring some attention to a county park that could end up closing without proper funding.

The river narrowed, and the propeller scraped the bottom.

The watercraft jerked back, forcing her body forward. Her butt bumped off the bench and onto the fiberglass floor.

Shit.

She quickly climbed back up, grabbing the handle as she slowed the boat. Holding her breath, she leaned over. The brackish water was too dark to see the bottom, but she was definitely hitting it. Turning the vessel around, she pulled out her phone. GPS should help guide her back to the beginning, and she could start all over.

No freaking service.

Of course, not.

The boat bucked, and the engine bounced up as the prop ground into the silt. The dockhand had warned her that the tide was going out and that she needed to make it to the docks at the campsite within the next few hours. That there were areas in the river that got so low, she could get stuck.

She let out a long sigh as she scanned the area. It appeared she'd managed to find a sandbar. All she needed to do was push the boat off it and maneuver around the port side to be able to get back into the broader part of the waterway.

The roar of an engine caught her attention. She glanced north and saw *him* heading her way.

Wonderful. Not how she wanted to see Philip for the first time on this trip. The entire idea had been to impress the hell out of him, not need him to *save* her. That would only perpetuate the concept that she was a high-maintenance female, who only cared about her next mani-pedi.

She glanced at her toes and groaned. She was overdue.

"Looks like you've gotten yourself into a little bit of trouble." Philip sat behind a steering wheel in a watercraft that looked like a blow-up toy with a motor. It reminded her of the tender on her father's yacht that the deck crew used to taxi them back and forth from anchor to port.

"It's just a little sandbar type thing. I can get out and push it and jump back in." Yeah. She'd seen people do that on the private beach by her parents' place all the time. It shouldn't be too hard as long as Mr. Sexy Ranger Man stopped staring at her with amusement dancing in his teal-blue eyes.

"Ella, you don't want to do that." He shook his head. "The bottom isn't like the beach. It's more like quicksand. You'll sink to your knees."

She shivered. The only time she wanted to be caked in mud was at the spa.

"The mistake you made, besides passing the campgrounds a half-hour ago, was turning around back there. Had you just backed out, you would have been fine."

Thanks for the lecture. "What do you suggest I do now? I'm supposed to go live to my followers…"— she glanced at her Apple Watch—"in a little over an hour. I'm doing a whole series on different parks and some of the history they have in our community, along with their great outdoor activities."

He covered his mouth, and his shoulders moved up and down.

She scowled. "I don't see what's so funny."

"I'm sorry." He cleared his throat. "I've seen some of your YouTube videos, and camping on an island that you won't be able to get off until the tide comes back in doesn't seem like your cup of tea. Especially all alone. Unless we had some sort of holistic yoga healing studio with a juice bar." He pointed to the sky. "And the storm's rolling in."

"Well, if you think that, you haven't been watching enough of my live feeds." She tilted her head. Dark clouds hovered a few miles away. The weather app mentioned it would most likely rain, but that was all supposed to happen north of Martin County. "That's all moving out to sea."

"If you say so," Philip said. He maneuvered his boat, pushing his bow up against hers. "Hop on." He held out his hand.

"What about all my stuff? The boat? We can't just leave it here."

"We're not going to." He patted the bench. "Think you can manage putting this in reverse and hang out in the open water over there while I unstick the rental?"

"Of course." Instead of taking the help he offered, she stepped from her vessel. "Oh, shit." She lunged forward, flinging into his arms. She dug her fingernails into his thick shoulders.

"Well, hello, there." He groaned, wrapping one arm around her and stretching out the other as he grabbed the steering wheel. His body twisted as his butt landed with a thud on the bench.

Straddling his lap, she jerked her head back and swallowed. His piercing gaze tore through her like the Blue Angels soaring through the sky. Her breath caught in her throat. She'd known Philip since high school, and while he was the heir to Prince Technologies, the biggest tech conglomerate in the United States, she'd never known him to be anything but rough, rugged, and a man all about the outdoors. She doubted if he even knew how to use a computer, other than to check his email—if he even *had* email.

He brushed her hair from her face. "Are you okay?" His tongue peeked out from between his plump lips and brushed at them with a thick, broad stroke.

"I should be asking you that." Her heart hammered in her chest. She tilted her head, leaning in. It couldn't be this easy to land her prince, could it?

He chuckled. "I think I'll live," he said, lifting her from his legs and gently setting her on the bench. He leaned over her, his hot breath tickling the side of her face as he tapped the throttle, nudging the boat forward until it hit bottom. "Remember what I said, just hang out in the middle out there. I'll be right back."

She let out a puff of air as she curled her fingers around the steering wheel, then backed out into the open water and put the engine in neutral. She watched as Philip's biceps bulged as he lifted the motor, setting it down with only part of the prop in the water. He tugged at the pull cord. Immediately, brown liquid spurted, churning up the filthy water. Birds squawked and flew from their branches into the blue sky.

He revved the engine in reverse as he stood on the back corner, rocking left and right until the vessel came loose and floated under the thick, lush branches. "I'm going to drive out to the other side. Stay right there."

As much as she wanted to leave, she didn't know how to get back to civilization.

2

*P*hilip finished his fried egg sandwich and stared at the storm brewing over the ocean. There were only five campsites on the island, and everyone had canceled because of the weather. All except Ella.

He rinsed out his coffee mug, glancing over at her tent, and bit back a laugh as she bent over, fumbling with a couple of poles that didn't go where she was trying to put them.

What the hell was she doing out here? Ella was the daughter of Darius Kane, a real estate mogul worth billions. An investor who took pride in making sure his precious, one-and-only baby girl didn't have to lift a finger if she didn't want to.

As it turned out, her idea of making a difference in the world had been to become some kind of social media influencer—whatever the fuck that was. He'd once watched a couple of her videos on some bike-a-thon she'd participated in for charity. He had to admit, she was highly entertaining, mostly because she could barely ride a bike to save her adorable little ass.

In more recent shows, she'd helped to raise thousands of dollars for various causes, which actually impressed him and made him want to get to know the real Ella. Only he didn't think she'd ever consider him the catch of the county. No. Ella dated men who enjoyed five-hundred-dollar bottles of wine, not guys who preferred to catch and clean their own dinner.

He strolled across the campground. If he didn't help her now, she would be soaked in the middle of the night. "That doesn't go there," he said.

She jumped, hitting her head on the top of the tarp drooping over the front of the tent. The fabric twisted around her body, and she stumbled backward.

"I gotcha." He stretched out his arms and snatched her up before she face-planted on the wooden platform. Unfortunately, her sleeping quarters toppled over into a heaping pile of nylon. He steadied her while he unraveled the material.

"I'm such a klutz."

"Yeah, you are." He took her chin between his thumb and forefinger. All through high school, he'd had the hots for Ella. Unfortunately, she belonged to the captain of the football team, who happened to be Philip's best friend. "You also suck at camping."

"The directions make no sense. I'm supposed to be streaming this live. My followers genuinely want to see what Black Park Island looks like when the tide goes out, but there's no cell reception."

"I have a Wi-Fi booster." He tucked a strand of her soft, light brown hair behind her ear. The rest cascaded down to the center of her back. He'd gone off to college, and when he returned to Jupiter, Florida, she and his buddy had broken up, leaving it open for Phillip to make his move. Only he and Ella couldn't be more opposite. They had only two things in common: their fathers were rich, and they'd grown up in the same neighborhood. Other than that, she could in no way fit into his world—as made obvious by the mess she'd made of the tent.

Her long, thick lashes lowered over her almond-colored eyes. They reminded him of gold sparkling in the river as the sun rays shone brightly, cutting through the water.

"You mean I could connect to the internet?"

14

He nodded as he ran his hands down her forearms, enjoying her soft, silky skin. She had a lightness about her that he'd always admired. She wasn't your typical trust-fund kid, but she certainly wasn't earning a living on her own, that was for damn sure.

"It can still be a little spotty. But, yes. If you go over to the outdoor kitchen area, you should be able to pull it up. The password is *alligator*. You won't be able to go too far from that spot, but it should work. I'll fix your tent." He took her hands in his, noting the long fingernails and the pretty, sparkly pink nail polish. Talk about a fish out of water. The poor girl was in for a rough night.

"You don't mind?"

"Not at all. Go, do your thing before it gets dark."

"Thanks." She grabbed a bag and jogged off with her hair bouncing over her shoulders as if she were in a shampoo commercial.

He turned his attention from Ella and her long, tan legs to the tent that a five-year-old could pitch with nothing but a diagram. His mother would smack him upside the head for how much enjoyment he hoped to get out of watching Ella attempt to start a fire and make herself camp food.

However, the weather still concerned him. The

radar had these storms hovering just a mile north of the campsite through the early hours of the morning. Still, the local meteorologist believed it would expand to include the campground and could even create tornados. His little island wouldn't necessarily be the safest place.

The pop-up took him all of ten minutes to set up. Since he figured she'd probably botch blowing up her air mattress, he did that for her as well, noting that she hadn't bothered to take off the price tags on her brand-new equipment.

He leaned against the picnic table, folded his arms, and took in the view, trying not to laugh as Ella held up her cell and walked around the kitchen area as she pointed to different sections on the island. Her voice rose a few sweet octaves as she detailed her adventures, which included getting her boat stuck in the mud—although she took a few liberties with the story to make it more exciting for her viewers.

She did a little hip-hop dance three-sixty, blowing kisses at the camera when he noticed she was wearing a pair of strappy sandals and about to tiptoe herself right into a sand pile filled with red ants that would have a field day with her tasty skin.

He pushed from the table. "Ella," he called.

There was no way this ended well. "Watch where you're stepping."

"Oh, and you all get to meet Ranger Philip Prince. He's certainly proven to be my Prince Charming today." Her foot landed in the tall sand pile, and hundreds of red ants went wild, clinging to her sweet skin. "Ouch. What the heck?" She looked down and started kicking her foot. "Oh, my God. They're everywhere." She flicked and slapped at her calf.

"Step away from the sand and stop moving so much." He raced to the sink and filled a pot with water. "Relax."

But she didn't listen. Nope. She continued wiggling, her arms flailing wildly like a bird. She took two wrong steps and tripped on a root, and now her adorable ass was covered in sand.

And red ants.

Quickly, he doused her foot before hoisting her off the ground. Setting her on the counter, he started brushing her thighs, hips, and anywhere he saw the nasty little biters.

"Those are horrible creatures." She wiggled, slapping at herself. "Crap. They're inside my shorts."

He laughed. Hard. He knew he shouldn't, but

he just couldn't help himself. Turning the faucet back on, he covered his hands in water and rid her bare skin of any insect he could find. "You might want to take a quick shower and put on fresh clothes."

She held up her phone as she wiggled left and right. "Okay, my lovelies. You heard the man. Besides, these ants are making a meal of my tushy. Now, don't forget to go to the county website and click on the donation button. We don't want to lose this beautiful park. Until next time, take a step out of your comfort zone and into a brand new you."

"You were still recording?" Philip lifted her into his arms, carrying her toward the showers. He contemplated taking her to his quarters. But if he did that, he'd try to put the moves on her, and that wasn't a path he thought he should travel. They were just too opposite. Besides, a woman like Ella wouldn't want to spend a few days to a week out here. The only thing to influence would be the wildlife.

"The show must go on." She continued squirming in his arms. "Would you bring over my bag?"

"Will do." He kicked open the door and set her down inside the shower area.

She immediately undid the top button of her shorts.

He groaned. This was going to be a long night.

3

*E*lla sat on the wood stump in front of the open fire and twisted her damp hair up into a messy bun on the top of her head. In the distance, lightning lit up the sky like fireworks. The wind picked up, rustling the leaves and bringing with it a sudden chill. Shadowy clouds covered the stars and the moon, making the island eerily dark.

The world thought Ella didn't have to lift a finger because her father handed her whatever she wanted on a silver platter. For a long time, she would have agreed with that assessment, owning it as if she were proud of the fact. However, a few months ago, she'd overheard Philip at a party, talking about how shallow she appeared. She had to admit, he had a point. She used her influence on things like lifestyle brands and posh travel spots. Philip had gone as far as to say how someone with her reach could really do some good in the world.

But what? And that's when she decided to slowly change her focus from a self-absorbed, privileged, rich girl to a young woman trying to figure out who she was. She'd create awareness about the issues of her community and take charge of her life. Ever since she'd listened to Philip knock her down a peg, she'd set out to change what topics she covered in her videos. She also wanted to show Philip that there was more to her than *sparkles and rainbows wrapped in a pretty box that had little to no substance*. His words.

She twisted the cap of her water and took a long swig. Scanning the campsite, she wondered where he'd ducked off to. In her research about Black Park Island, she'd read that the rangers lived onsite. What fascinated her even more, was that back in the early forties, a trapper named Conrad owned the island. After he married, he dammed off the river, making it so no one could come to the island unless he wanted them to. Conrad, his wife, and their two children lived here, isolated from the world until Conrad died in nineteen sixty-nine. His wife, who later wrote a book about their life, opened up the river and sold the land to the county, where it became part of the park system.

Unfortunately, it was currently on the chopping block. The county might sell this piece of property to a privately owned establishment, which could potentially upset not only the wildlife balance but rich history, as well.

She shivered as the first raindrops hit her body. They were large, and they stung almost as much as the stupid ant bites had. The wind howled, and in a second, the sky opened up and drenched her, dousing the fire in the pit.

Quickly, she climbed into her tent, zipping it closed. Darkness engulfed her senses. She fumbled to find the battery-powered lantern. The wind lifted the sides of the canvas, rattling the metal stakes used to tie it down. Thunder shook the earth, while a lightning bolt snaked across the sky, lighting up the inside of her tent as if she were the film of an X-ray.

"Ella. Come on." Out of nowhere, Phillip stuck his head inside her tent.

She jumped. "You scared me."

"Sorry," he said, reaching inside and curling his arms under her legs and back, lifting her into the air.

"What are you doing?"

"It's not safe for you to be out here right now." He took off, sloshing through the mud. Large raindrops smashed into her face like water balloons exploding on impact. "According to the Storm Prediction Center, we've got the perfect mixture of wind and pressure to create a tornado."

She tucked her face into his neck, trying to peek open one eye. He ran to the other side of the grounds and ducked behind the community building before moving down a short, wooded path to a log cabin.

No. More like a log *house* right out of the pages of *Adirondack Living*. Wrong part of the country, as Florida tended to go with stucco and pastels, but it worked for the rugged ranger.

He kicked open the front door and set her feet on the hardwood floor. "We're going to have to hunker down in here." He quickly locked the door, took her by the hand, and practically yanked her arm right out of its socket. He snagged something off the table in the kitchen before shoving her through his bedroom and into a big bathroom. "Get in the bathtub."

"Excuse me?"

"It's the safest place." He held up a computer

tablet and tapped the screen. "A tornado just touched down two miles from here. Now, do as I say."

She climbed into his impressive bathtub. It wasn't your everyday, run-of-the-mill bachelor cabin.

Thump!

"What was that?" She hugged her knees tight to her chest.

"Probably a tree hitting the ranger station." He stepped in behind her, stretching his legs out on either side of hers and drawing her back to his hard body. With his arms wrapped around her, he tapped on his gadget.

"You know how to use that?"

He chuckled. "You should see all the techie things I have in my office. It takes a lot to keep this island and park running. Besides, how do you think I found you? Didn't you notice how far off the beaten path you'd gone today?"

"I guess." She glanced at the ceiling as the house vibrated and shook. It was like being in the black and white part of *The Wizard of Oz*. She half expected to look out the window and see a woman riding her bike with a little dog in the basket. "So, how did you find me?"

"All the rentals have trackers on them."

"That's very big brother-ish." She dropped her head back onto his strong shoulder and inhaled sharply. He smelled like fresh fog mixed with a salty sunrise. She glanced up at him. His blue eyes electrified the room but calmed her soul. The wind tore through the trees outside, and desire ripped through her body like wild horses roaming free on the beach. "I'm glad you found me."

"I am, too." He kissed her nose.

The house rattled, knocking a picture off the wall. A deep howl echoed through the night.

"What the hell is that noise?" she asked.

"I'm guessing that's a tornado." He set the tablet on the floor and hugged her close. "According to the radar, it's going to skip right over us and then move out to sea."

The sound of glass shattering scratched at her ears like fingernails on a chalkboard. The porcelain tub vibrated.

She clutched at his shirt, trembling harder and faster than anything around her. "This was a stupid idea," she mumbled. "Why did I think I could impress you, of all people?"

He rested his chin on the top of her head and rubbed his hands up and down her back. "I thought you were here to do one of your influencer pieces on....on...something."

"I am. And part of my new social media strategy is to tell people to go after what they want. And I want you. Only you seldom leave this island, and when you do, you never give me the time of day. All you do is make fun of me. I just wanted to show you that there is more to me than what you see on social media."

He coughed. "I see."

She buried her face in the fabric of his shirt. The roar of the wind sounded more like a freight train. But the shaking of the house slowed as did the horrifying noise. A few long moments passed as the loud crack of thunder was replaced by deafening silence. The only thing she could hear was the pounding of her heart.

He tilted her head. "You did all this to get my attention?"

Nodding, she let out a puff of air. "Well, that and I wanted people to know about the island and give to the fund to keep it from becoming privately owned."

"I'm impressed." His mouth covered hers in a tender kiss. He parted her lips, his hot tongue finding every crevice, sending the kinds of signals to the rest of her body that meant she might not be sleeping alone tonight, much less in a tent.

A deep moan formed in her gut and vibrated into her throat.

"Ella, I've always noticed you," he said.

"But you think I'm a spoiled brat who hasn't a clue about the world."

"You're right. I did *think* that. But you're changing my mind." He lifted his tablet and touched the screen. "The worst has passed." He stood, helping her from the tub.

She adjusted her ponytail and looked around at the masculine room with its kingsize bed and wood headboard under a skylight. "You really live out here?"

He chuckled. "It's a shared space between all the rangers. There are three of us, and we rotate our schedule. When I'm working, I live here." He adjusted the battery-powered lantern and pulled out some towels from the closet. "You're soaking wet." He wrapped the terrycloth around her body and heaved her to his chest. "So, what do you think about roughing it?"

"I kind of like it, minus the ants. I really could have done without those." She wrapped her arms around his broad frame. "I know that, for a long time, I lived in the lands of unicorns and rainbows

27

where Daddy fixed everything with his credit card. But a lot has changed since we were in high school. I'm not shallow. I do have substance, and I'm trying to use what I've created with my social media following to promote awareness and change."

"I've noticed."

She cocked her head. "You've really been watching my videos?"

"I started to when I heard what you did for that firefighter and his family a few months ago. It was pretty amazing what you accomplished." He leaned in and pressed his mouth over hers for a long, passionate kiss with the promise of many more to come. "I still don't understand what you do. Or how it all works. But I can appreciate a good cause."

"That means a lot coming from you," she said.

"I do have a couple of questions, though."

"Yeah? What's that?" she asked. Butterflies filled her gut as she watched him pull back the comforter on the massive bed.

"Are you willing to give camping a real try? With me? I have a few days off next week. I thought I'd do a little fishing. We could even sleep on the boat. It's a far cry from a yacht, but it's comfortable enough."

"Oh, boy. That would be stepping out of my

comfort zone," she said.

"Staying over on the boat, or sleeping with me?"

Tugging her ponytail free, she took the towel to her wet hair, giving it a good scrub before tossing the bath sheet on the chair in the corner. She toyed with the hem of her shirt, lifting it over her head.

He growled.

"I'm hoping the latter is more than comfortable. Actually, terms like *explosive*, *mind-blowing*, *the best I've ever had*, all stick out in my brain," she said.

"We could turn the boating adventure into a social media influencer thingy by doing a piece on manatees or something."

She shed her shorts and jumped between the sheets in only her bra and panties. "Anyone ever tell you that you talk too much?"

"Can't say anyone has ever complained about that." He slipped under the covers and pulled her tight against him. "You're not exactly who I thought you were, and I'm going to enjoy getting to know the real you."

"I always knew someday my ranger would come."

One corner of his lips tipped up, and then he turned serious. His warm lips caressed hers like a paintbrush stroking the canvas for the first time with the promise of something beautiful. His hands massaged her body like a master sculptor creating the perfect piece of art.

She belonged in his arms. And she would remain there forever.

The End

ITS ALWAYS BEEN YOU

IT'S ALWAYS BEEN YOU

A Valentine's Day Short Story

by
USA Today Bestselling Author
JEN TALTY

To Stacey Wilk. Thanks for sharing your car rides. Your friendship means the world to me. You truly are the sister I choose.

1

"Can I get anything else for you?" Shelly Ambrose placed the single rose in a plastic sleeve and tied a red ribbon around the center, trying not to stare at the dashing new neighbor with the sexy eyes. She told herself she was ready for someone to ask her out on a date, and considering her favorite holiday was coming up, maybe she'd give it a go.

It wasn't like Axel was going to waltz into the shop and do something quirky or romantic, which is why she'd broken up with him.

"This should do the trick. Thanks," Alan said as he handed her a twenty-dollar bill. "So, do you have a special Valentine?"

"I'm flying solo this year so far." Shelly made the change, doing her best to smile as sweetly as she could. "But it's obvious you have one." She handed him his change.

He laughed. "This is for my niece. It's her dance recital tonight, and I don't want to be the idiot who comes empty-handed."

"You're a sweet uncle."

He nodded. "Speaking of sweet. Any idea where I can get a box of chocolate-covered strawberries?"

"If you have time to go downtown, The Fruit and Nut Tree has a spectacular lineup of all sorts of things," she said. "And it's all fresh. You can't go wrong. Show them the receipt from here, and they will give you a discount."

The front door swung open and in strolled Alex Giovanni, all six foot two of him, wearing his fatigues which he made look like a three-piece suit. He shoved his hands in his pockets and smiled that damn sensual smile that sent her senses into a frenzy.

"Thanks. I really appreciate it." Alan leaned across the counter. "Hey, would you like to get a cup of coffee with me sometime?" Alan asked.

"Sure. I'd like." Her heart thumped in her throat. She kept telling herself she was ready to date. It had been six months since she'd moved out of Axe's townhouse. Three months since they'd had any conversation. Of course, he'd been deployed for those months, but she was ready to move on.

At least that's what her head kept trying to tell her heart.

If only she didn't still love the jerk. Oh, who was she kidding. Axel wasn't a jerk, far from it. But he couldn't do the smallest of things for her, like celebrating Valentine's Day, and she'd told him if he didn't change, she'd leave.

She stuck to her word when, six months ago, he didn't do anything other than take her out on the boat for their anniversary.

"Great. I'll be in touch." Alan nodded to Axel as he meandered out the door.

"You're really going to go out with that guy?" Axel asked.

Thank God Kendra, her longest and best friend, entered from the back room. "Axel, you're home," Kendra said as she rubbed her very round belly. "When did you get back?"

"Landed about two hours ago," Axel said. "You're looking very pregnant."

"I'm well aware of that fact," Kendra said. "I'm all done. Are we ready to close up?"

"Just about." Shelly held Axel's stare. God, how she missed being in his arms. The way he smelled. How he kissed her good morning and winked at her every night. She missed everything about him, except his inability to give her one tiny little thing. "Did you come in here for a reason? Maybe to buy some flowers for someone?"

Axel had the audacity to crack a smile.

"Of course not, because you put down the toilet seat, and that should be enough," she said, letting out a long breath. "Why are you here?"

"I certainly didn't come to have the same argument that we had the night you moved out. I thought maybe, just maybe, we could talk about things. Talk about us."

Shelly shook her head. She'd wasted two years of her life with Axel Giovanni. Of course, of those two years, she'd only spent maybe a total of eight months of them actually in his presence. But that hadn't been the problem. She understood that being in the Navy meant he'd often be deployed, especially because of his role as a SEAL. That didn't bother her at all. Her father had also been a SEAL. She knew and actually loved the lifestyle. She spent her childhood moving from one naval base to the next. She understood the military way of life. She could get on board with that. Hell, she had only been involved with servicemen. But what got under her skin had been the way he treated her feelings and her desires. How he totally disregarded the only thing she asked him to change about himself.

She wanted romance.

Not a lot, but she needed the little things.

If only he could have left her romantic notes on the vanity before he'd left for the base on their anniversary or on Valentine's Day. It didn't have to be a creative poem. All he had to do was put a heart on it. Maybe say he loved her. A smiley face would have done the trick. Not once in the two years she'd dated him did he ever send her flowers or chocolates on Valentine's Day. At the very least, he could have taken her to dinner. But no, Axel couldn't be bothered to take the time to do the tiniest gesture that most would consider considerate. Nope. His idea of being a good boyfriend was putting the toilet seat down.

Or the fact that he was a good cook and never expected her to have dinner on the table when he came home, much less do the dishes. He did his own laundry, including the ironing of his shirts, as well as hers. He also knew how to make the bed, and not once did he complain about all her throw pillows.

She appreciated all those things about Axel. So, why did he dig his boots into the ground when she asked for a few cliché romantic actions on Valentine's Day and anniversaries?

"There is no us anymore," she said.

"I don't believe that." He closed the gap between them. "You still love me."

Oh, how she wished that wasn't true. Better yet, she wished he would have said he still loved her, but that would be too much to ask.

"I'm back for a couple of weeks. I'm going to show you."

Before she had a chance to say anything, he turned on a dime and marched right out of her floral shop.

"Oh, my God. That man makes me nuts." Shelly gathered up her things as quickly as she could. She just wanted to get home, put her feet up, and have some wine. But she wouldn't even be able to do that for long because she had a stupid engagement party to go to.

"I want to know what he's going to show you because he didn't make that clear at all," Kendra said.

"Probably that he's still an arrogant, stubborn man who thinks romance went out with woman's liberation." Shelly pulled the store door closed and locked it up for the night. "So glad he and I are done."

"Maybe, but you're still in love with him," Kendra said as she strolled down Beach Shores Drive in a military neighborhood outside of San Diego across the Bay from the Naval Amphibious Base Coronado.

Shelly's father had become a Navy SEAL instructor ten years ago, and this had been the longest she'd lived anywhere. She'd seen Navy men come and go, and she always thought she'd be following one of them to bases across the globe. Actually, the second she'd met Axel, she knew she'd found the one.

Until he wasn't.

"Being in love with someone isn't enough," Shelly said.

Kendra patted her belly. "I disagree. You're being as stubborn and childish as he is. Axel hasn't once asked you to change a single thing about yourself, and it's not like he has some horrible habit like drinking too much or gambling."

"It's not about that, and you know it. Love is about compromise and mutual respect. He has none for me, or he'd understand why his actions are so hurtful."

"So he's not romantic, who cares. He's still got a big heart, and we miss having you both over at the same time."

43

"I'm sorry I broke up our perfect foursome, but I can't be with him if he's not going to consider some of my feelings. And it goes beyond what I'm asking for myself." They stopped in front of Shelly's condo building. It was nice to be able to walk to work, but she missed the townhouse on the beach that she used to share with Axel. It was a shame that it went unused when he was deployed. "We were starting to talk about getting married and having kids." Shelly smiled as she placed her hands on her friend's swollen stomach. "Axel just doesn't think about his actions, or lack of actions, and how they make others feel, and I won't be in a relationship with a man who won't at least acknowledge that he's heard me. I mean, what kind of an example would that be for kids?"

"I swear to God, woman, you watch way too much *Dr. Phil.*" Kendra pointed at the bench in the lobby. "You've got a package."

Shelly glanced around the lobby. Usually deliveries were left at the desk. She picked up the box. "It's from The Fruit and Nut Tree in downtown." She searched the package for a shipping label, but there wasn't one.

"Who's it from?"

"I don't know, but whoever sent it to me hand-delivered it." She hit the elevator button five times, willing the machine to get to the lobby faster. "Maybe one of my neighbors left it for me as a thank you for leaving all the leftover fresh flowers in the lobby since I moved here."

"Or maybe it's from Alan."

"I doubt that. No way did he have enough time. Besides, he doesn't know where I live," Shelly said, but part of her was hoping, just a little a bit, that Alan managed to pick her something sweet from her favorite sweet shop.

The elevator doors dinged open. Her heart hammered in her chest as she tapped her foot on the tile floor. Excitement she hadn't felt in years swirled around in her belly.

"Aren't you going to open it?"

"Yup." Shelly made a beeline for her apartment. Once inside her kitchen, she pulled down a wine glass and poured some white she'd been chilling in the fridge. She took a big gulp before fiddling with the edges of the package. If it was from Alan, she'd have to admit, she'd be more interested in that cup of coffee and maybe upping it to some wine.

This was exactly the kind of thing she wanted in a man.

She pulled the top of the box off. The note tickled her fingertips. Holding her breath, she slipped the piece of paper from the envelope and read the printed words out loud.

"Three days to Valentine's Day? Will you be my sweetheart?"

"That's it? That's all it says?" Kendra asked.

"That's it."

"Looks like someone has a secret admirer."

Shelly smiled. Her heart melted like milk chocolate left under the warm summer sun. Whoever her secret admirer was, he understood the meaning of romance, and she would enjoy meeting him. Hopefully, he'd reveal himself soon.

2

"Well, hello there, Shelly. You look pretty tonight," Maverick said.

Shelly lifted her wine glass and clanked it against his beer. "Thank you. You dress up nice." She'd known Maverick for about ten years. He'd started his career as a SEAL stationed in Coronado but had been transferred shortly after. She'd only gone out on a few dates with him, but she'd been pretty smitten with him back in the day. Then about a year ago, he'd returned, but she'd been living with Axel.

"I've always liked that dress on you."

She glanced down at the black-and-red floral dress she'd had for years. It had been one of her favorites. It was a classic piece that would never go out of style. "Flattery might get you places, but you don't have to lie."

"You wore that dress when I took you to Ameil's for Valentine's Day," Maverick said.

"Even I don't remember that I wore this dress on that date." She smiled. Maverick had been a sappy kind of boyfriend. Sweet, but over the top and often not all that genuine. Sometimes she felt like he was doing it just so she'd feel obligated to invite him up, which never happened. "It was a long time ago."

"I have to admit, I was shocked to hear about you and Axel."

She shrugged. "It wasn't meant to be." It had gotten easier and easier to keep the tears from stinging the corners of his eyes every time someone brought up her breakup in public.

Maverick shook his head. "Everyone thought the two of you would be getting married by now."

"That's never going to happen," she said.

"Then would it be in poor taste if I asked you out?" He winked.

"Oh no, you don't," Jet said as he draped his arm over her shoulder. "You had your chance ten years ago. Give someone else an opportunity."

Oh, good grief. All she needed now was for a

couple of SEALs to get into a pissing contest over her.

"I'm not an opportunity or some kind of prize, fellas," she said, patting Jet on the chest. "I need to use the little girl's room. I'll see you two later." It was time for her to hit the road, but first she had to get her bag, which she'd left in the kitchen.

She rounded the corner and paused midstep.

"Having a good time?" Axel leaned against the kitchen counter looking all sexy in his jeans and dark V-neck shirt.

"It's been a fun party." Shelly remembered the first time she'd ever laid eyes on Axel. He'd been playing volleyball on the beach with a bunch of other SEALs when he waltzed over to her and boldly told her that he planned on taking her out to dinner that night. When she told her father who she was going on a date with, her father more than enjoyed showing up at her apartment to give Axel a hard time.

Only Axel held his own.

Another reason she fell head over heels in love with him.

"They make a cute couple," Axel said.

"I'm still shocked that Tyler actually pulled the trigger and asked Erica to marry him," she admitted. "He came to the shop the day he proposed and bought all the roses I had in the store."

"That's your kind of proposal," Axel said. "Although, I heard he nearly botched the entire thing."

"Yeah, putting roses with thorns on a bed you plan on seducing a woman in isn't really a good idea." Shelly laughed. "But he said it was still very romantic."

"But you probably thought it would have been better if it was done on Valentine's Day, right?"

She rolled her eyes. "No. Not necessarily."

Axel took her hand and raised it to his full lips. "I still don't understand why you need that one day so much when I've always been a gentleman. Haven't I always treated you with the utmost respect? I buy you gifts on your birthday, which I've never forgotten. Isn't this considered a little bit romantic?"

She yanked her hand away. "You don't understand and worse, you're still not hearing me."

He wrapped his arms around her, crushing her chest into his. "I hear you. I've always heard you. But you've never once asked me why I don't want to celebrate Valentine's Day." Firmly, he pressed his lips against hers, giving her mouth a quick sweep with his warm tongue that tasted like whiskey and chocolate cake.

Pounding her fist into his chest, she struggled to break off the kiss.

"I love you, Shelly. That's never going to change. And neither am I. Give me a chance to explain why those things that mean more to you than our relationship isn't in my wheelhouse, and if you still want to call it quits with me, I'll walk away and never bother you again."

Before she had a chance to say anything, five other people entered the kitchen. Next thing she knew, Axel was outside smoking a cigar, sipping whiskey, and telling dirty jokes with all his SEAL buddies, and she was getting into an Uber.

She opened her purse to find her keys, and instead, she found a single candied rose with a typed note.

Her heart skipped a couple of beats, and when it resumed, it pounded out of control at the base of her throat, making it nearly impossible to swallow. She held the envelope up between her shaky fingers. Who could have slipped this into her purse?

More importantly, who were the single men at the party?

Axel. Jet. Maverick. Benning. Cannon.

No Alan.

And she could rule out Axel, even though he'd been close to her purse at the end of the evening. But who knew how many of the other single men had been through the kitchen?

However, she had to ask who would know which purse was hers? Axel never noticed shit like that. Another thing that bothered her.

Maverick made the most sense. Then maybe Benning. He was quiet, but he noticed every little detail, something that her father really appreciated at work but drove him batshit crazy off the base.

God, not knowing who was leaving her things was going to make her insane. She pulled out her phone.

Shelly: I'm five minutes from my apartment. Where are you?

Kendra: Sitting with my feet up while Houston rubs them, why?

Shelly: I think I got another note from my secret admirer, but I don't want to open it alone.

Kendra: I'll have Houston open the front door. Just walk on in.

Shelly: Thanks. Just pulled into the circle.

Another nice thing about living in this particular building was her best friend and her husband rented the penthouse. Of course, Kendra came from a shit ton of money and didn't need her job at the floral shop, and Houston could retire from the military, but Houston recently took a position just under Shelly's father, and Kendra would leave her position after the baby was born, but she keeps saying she'll be back.

And that was fine with Shelly.

She raced through the door and into the family room where Houston greeted her with a glass of wine and a tray of cheese.

"Oh, my God. You didn't have to do that," she said.

"My wife would have my head if I didn't." He bent and kissed Kendra. "I'm off to bed. Don't stay up too late."

"I won't be here long, I promise." Shelly made herself comfortable on the sofa, tucking her feet under her butt. "This time I got a candy rose and this note." She placed it on Kendra's lap. "Will you read it?"

"Sure," Kendra said with a little too much excitement. She ripped open the envelope. *"Wow. You look amazing tonight. But you could make a flannel shirt look like a wedding dress. I hope you'll be my Valentine. I have a great night planned for us. I'll be in touch Valentine's Day morning with the details on where to meet me. Love, Your Personal Secret Admirer."*

"It can't be Alan because he wasn't at the

party." Shelly tossed her head back on the sofa. "I'm thinking it's Maverick, but I'm kind of hoping it's Benning."

"He's so socially awkward, though," Kendra said.

"That's what makes this so bizarrely romantic."

"If you say so." Kendra leaned forward and handed her the note. "Let me ask you one thing though. What if this is all coming from Axel? What would you do then?"

"It's not him. I know that for a fact." Shelly laughed, but her pulsed raced. She wanted to believe Axel could change, but she knew he hadn't. "He kissed me tonight and told me I should have asked him why he doesn't do Valentine's Day or some of the other stuff. He actually thinks we should talk about it."

"You never asked him for a specific reason?" Kendra asked with a raised brow.

"Of course. I mean I asked him why he didn't celebrate Valentine's Day, and he said he showed me he loved me all the time. The first year we were together and I pressed, he got angry, so last year, I didn't press. I just got mad and moved out a few months later."

"You two broke up for the dumbest reasons," Kendra said.

"All he had to do was take me to dinner, get me a rose, and put a chocolate on my pillow. What's the big deal?"

"The big deal is you're both stubborn. I think you should hear him out."

"I will, but not until after I find out who my secret admirer is. I've never had one before. I've always wanted one. It's so romantic and for it to be on Valentine's Day." She hugged herself. This is all she'd ever wanted. Just a little attention from Cupid. "I'm not going to let Axel's return ruin this chance for me."

"I don't see how talking to the man is ruining anything. Besides, do you really see yourself dating any of the single SEALs from the party tonight?"

"You never know. Stranger things have happened."

3

*S*helly did her best to keep her disappointment from rising to the surface. It shouldn't matter that the entire day had gone by and she hadn't heard a single thing from her secret admirer. Well, the day hadn't ended yet. Maybe he'd left something at her apartment.

The bell over the door to the shop rang, and Axel stepped through. "Hey," he said. "How are you?"

"Fine. What can I do for you?" she asked, trying not to sound too annoyed, even though she knew she did.

"We need to talk."

"So you keep saying." She let out a long breath. No way did she want to do this now, but she knew him, and he wasn't going to let up.

"I know I said some pretty mean things when you moved out."

"Ya think?" She folded her arms across her chest and glared at him. Of course, she said her fair share of deplorable words meant to cut him where it could hurt him the most.

And it had been successful.

"I've had some time to think about things, and I want to apologize."

She closed her eyes for a brief moment. "For what exactly?" She'd been waiting for this moment for what seemed like forever, believing it would never come.

"Can we go for a walk? Or maybe go get a drink or something?" He tossed his hands to the sides.

She noticed he carried a small package. "What's that?"

"Oh. Sorry. I found this shoved halfway in your mailbox out front. Just has your name on it."

"Oh. Thanks." She raced around the counter and snagged the package, ripping it open. "It's taffy."

"You love that stuff," he said with a chuckle.

She nodded as she lifted the card, making sure there was no way in hell Axel could see the words on the page.

Do you have any clue as to who I might be? I suppose if you did, you'd call me out. Enjoy the taffy. Save a piece or two for me. Your Secret Admirer.

Everyone in town knew she had a thing for taffy. She left a small tray of it out on the counter at the shop, and she tended to give it as gifts to her vendors. It was her thing, so this gift didn't narrow down the potential suitors.

Two more days until Valentine's Day, and Shelly was doing her best to contain her excitement. Every time a man walked into the shop, she wondered, could that be him?

She stuffed the note in her back pocket before taking a piece of the taffy and popping it in her mouth.

"Who's it from?"

"Just a friend," she said. "I was just about to leave, so if you want to walk me home and talk, that would be fine."

"I'll take it," he said, holding the door open. "Can I have a piece?"

"Sure." She tossed him one of the vanilla ones, knowing he preferred that flavor. She stuffed a handful into her purse, leaving the rest in the drawer so she could savor them tomorrow while she contemplated who her admirer could possibly be.

Once she locked the door, she strolled along the sidewalk next to Axel. If they'd still been together, she would have looped her hand into his elbow and leaned into his strong frame. He would have pressed his warm lips on her temple and whispered something sweet in her ear.

He was romantic in every way except for the one way she needed most.

"What did you want to discuss with me?" She held on to her purse and kept her focus on the street ahead.

"Let's take a detour down by the docks, okay?"

"It's getting late, and I have to get up early."

"Just a half hour, that's all I ask." He pressed his hand on the small of her back and nudged her across the street.

She should protest harder, but it was rare that Axel groveled. Not that she could describe this as begging of any kind, but she did want to hear him out, if for no other reason than she was curious. "All right."

"Thank you." He bought them each a cup of decaf coffee before sitting down on a bench at the end of the pier. "I have a really big confession to make."

"Okay." She didn't like the sound of that.

"I lied to you about my parents."

The Styrofoam mug slipped from her fingers and dropped to the pavement. "Shit," she mumbled, jumping off the seat. Thankfully, the scalding liquid didn't come anywhere near her exposed skin. "What do you mean? You told me your parents died in a car accident when you were twelve and that your uncle raised you."

"My uncle did raise me. I didn't lie about that part. However, my parents are currently serving a life sentence with the possibility of parole for multiple murders."

"Holy fuck," she muttered. Her mouth went dry, and her pulse pounded in her throat. She tried to swallow but couldn't. "I didn't hear that correctly, did I?"

He pulled out his phone and tapped at the screen. "My uncle and I changed our names because it seemed to be the only way to get out from under the publicity and give me a chance at a normal life. I developed a story about my parents, and I stuck with it. But maybe once you see this, you'll understand why I don't do Valentine's Day or anniversaries." He handed her his cell.

"What am I looking at?"

"Just read." He set his coffee on the bench.

"You drink this. I'll go get myself another one. By the time I come back, you should be finished." Stuffing his hands in his pockets, he turned and strolled down the pier.

She sucked in a deep breath and started reading.

John and Brandi Hogan might go down in history as the most notorious killers in the country. Their crimes span over twelve years and potentially at least twenty victims.

Tears stung Shelly's eyes.

They considered themselves the Bonnie and Clyde of the twenty-first century. During an interview with the police, John said it all started when he wanted to give his wife the best Valentine's Day present ever, and the only thing he could think of was showing her the thrill of the kill. So he took her on her first hunt.

"Oh, my God." Shelly clutched her chest. His parents were dubbed the Cupid Killers, which was a horrible name. She remembered watching a documentary on them when she'd been in college and how horrified she'd been by the entire thing. Doing her best to control her breathing, she brought the phone back to her gaze.

From there, every Valentine's day and every wedding anniversary, the couple would find another young couple to kidnap, torture, rape, and murder.

Shelly dropped the phone to her lap and dipped her head back. Staring at the night sky, she swallowed a guttural sob. The sound of heavy boots caught her attention.

"You okay?" Axel asked.

"No," she said. "Is this some kind of twisted joke?" She didn't want to believe that Axel could be the product of such terrible people. Nor did she want to face the hell he must have gone through knowing what his parents had done.

"I wish. And I'd appreciate it if you didn't tell people."

"Does anyone know?"

He nodded. "My CO. Maverick..." He paused for a long moment. "Your father."

She bolted upright. "No fucking way. No way did he know this and not tell me."

Axel bent over and picked up his cell. "He just found out this morning. I thought I needed to tell him." Axel leaned against the railing and looked out over the ocean. "It's not that I can't be romantic, you know that. But my parents made such a big deal about Valentine's Day, more so than anniversaries. My mom used to tell me that when I was older, and I had a girl, she and my father would bring me into their little Valentine's Day game."

"I don't know what to say."

"There's nothing anyone can say. It's taken me a long time to know and believe I'm nothing like my parents. That genetics plays no role in how I've turned out."

She rested a hand on his forearm. "You're a good man."

"Thank you." He swiped at his eyes. "But it doesn't erase the shame. That said, I wanted you to know. Now let's get you home. I know it's a lot to take in."

"It is."

"And your father will want to hear from you."

They remained silent for the rest of the walk to her apartment. So many questions and yet she couldn't bring herself to ask a single one.

"Thank you for hearing me out." He kissed her temple. "When you're ready to talk more, let me know."

"I'm sorry I don't have more to say now."

"Don't be. I just tossed a lot at you."

She nodded.

"Good night, Shelly."

One of the things she wanted to ask him was why he let her walk out of his life six months ago. All he had to do was tell her the truth. This she could understand. This she could work with.

But no. He helped her pack her bags and called the moving truck.

Maybe he had a good reason for not wanting to celebrate the holiday, but he didn't love her enough to be honest with her about it.

4

One more day to Valentine's Day.

And Shelly almost didn't care.

Except her secret admirer had dropped off another gift, though she hadn't opened it yet.

"Thanks for your help, Daddy." She handed her father another box of roses that needed to be sorted and made into arrangements for last-minute purchases.

"My pleasure." He glanced over the rim of his glasses. "How are you holding up?"

"I'm still in shock."

"You and me both," her father said. "That was not the news I expected to hear from that young man when he showed up at the house. I half expected him to ask for your hand in marriage."

"Dad, you know we broke up."

"Yeah, well, your mother and I keep hoping you'll get back together." He reached out and took her by the hand. "Even knowing who his parents are."

She plopped herself on the stool behind the counter. "I Googled them last night. Big mistake."

"Yeah. Both on death row. Both lunatics."

"That's not the mistake part. I researched their son. Axel's name had been Jessie. They lived in suburbia, and he had what looked like a normal life. No one knew what his parents did. Not for years. And then when the world found out, poor Axel was ostracized. There were articles written about him that discussed the likelihood he would follow in his parents' path. And then I read the article where some kids bullied and beat him up."

"I read that one too," her father said. "But he's put all that behind him, which is why it was nearly impossible for him to tell you at all. But now the two of you can work on forgiveness."

She took the latest gift out and set it on the counter. "Six months ago, he told me not to let the door hit me in the ass on the way out. If he loved me as much as he said he does, he would have fought for me."

"I think he's fighting for you now."

"Might be a little too late." She waved the box. "I have a secret admirer."

"What does that have to do with you and Axel?"

"I know you really want me and Axel to work out, but right now I'm more interested in finding out who this is than dealing with him."

"All right." Her father put the roses down and made his way to the counter. "You don't say. Who do you think it is?"

"Well, I have my suspicions, but I can't be sure. Possibly Maverick. Maybe Benning. Could even be Jet, but I hope not. Hell, any of the single guys on the base."

"It's not Benning. He's been spending his nights with some girl that bartends at Joey's."

"That's a bummer. He's cute."

Her father rolled his eyes. "Are you going to open it?"

She pulled off the top and stared at a rose necklace with matching earrings. "Holy crap," she mumbled. "I saw this set at the jewelers down at the market. I thought about getting it but decided against it."

"When was that?"

"Yesterday on my way to work."

"Okay. I don't like an admirer that doubles as a stalker," her father said. "Is there a note?"

"Yes." She cleared her throat. *"It's over the top, I know. You won't believe when or where I bought it. But I will tell you tomorrow night. Your Secret Admirer."*

"I don't want you meeting this person alone. He sounds like a creeper."

"Dad. He's someone from the base. I know this for a fact because he was at the engagement party, and come on, let's face it; Maverick is a bit of a creeper."

"That is true, and this is something he would do in order to impress a girl." Her father waggled his finger. "But he does that for one reason only."

"Stop, Dad. I'm almost thirty years old, and I lived with a man, or have you forgotten?"

"Yeah, well, I wasn't overly thrilled with that at first either."

The bell over the door rattled and in waltzed Axel. "Good evening, sir."

"Axel. It's good to see you," her father said. "You're just in time to finish up with these roses. I'm going to head home and watch a movie with my lovely bride."

"Tell the Mrs. I said hello," Axel said with an outstretched hand.

Shelly kissed her father and then locked the door behind him. She would open the store early but would close by five, regular hours. If someone didn't have their Valentine's Day gift by then, that was their problem.

She had a date.

Of course, she had no idea where or when, but she'd find out soon enough.

"What is this?" Axel snagged the note before she could retrieve it.

"None of your business."

"Wow," he said. "A secret admirer. Is that where the taffy came from?"

"Yes," she admitted. She saw no reason to lie to Axel.

"Well, whoever this is, he knows you pretty well." He tapped the box. "You love roses. Taffy is your favorite. And you love everything that is Valentine's Day."

"I do," she said. "But I'll be totally honest with you. It's changed some since yesterday and what you told me."

He sat down at the small folding table with all the flowers and began arranging them like she'd shown him a few years ago. Not once did he ever say no to helping her. Not even on Valentine's Day when he'd make some last-minute deliveries for her, but he never did anything remotely romantic for her on that day.

But at least now she understood why.

"I didn't tell you so you'd change your point of view. I just decided I'd been an asshole long enough."

She joined him at the table and worked on the flowers. "Why didn't you tell me before I got so fed up I moved out?"

"I don't have an answer for that, other than fear."

"That's honest."

"I'm too late, aren't I?" Axel asked.

"I can't help but think you just didn't love me enough. I can't stop thinking about the day I left. We said some hurtful things to one another. I think this goes beyond your history."

He set a bunch of roses on the table. "I love you, Shelly. I know this admirer is giving you the mystery that you crave. But give me a chance. Have dinner with me tomorrow night. I'll do it right. I promise."

"I can't," she said, squeezing her eyes shut. "I'm sorry, Axel. Getting over you was the hardest thing I've ever had to do. I can't go back there."

He stood. "If you change your mind, meet me at the pier at five thirty. I've got a surprise for you."

Before she could say anything, he walked out the door.

5

VALENTINE'S DAY

*W*ith shaky fingers, Shelly opened the package that had been delivered to the shop. Tucked inside was a box of fudge and a note.

Shelly. It's time for us to meet. Well, we've already met. But it's time for me to reveal myself to you. I've left you hints along the way. Each gift should have been a clue. Look at them closely. Once you figure it out, you'll know where to meet me. That is if you still want to. Your Secret Admirer.

Oh fuck. Seriously?

She dropped her head to the counter.

"What's wrong?" Kendra asked.

Shelly pushed the note in front of her friend. "This is way too cryptic, even for me."

"Do you have all the gifts and notes here?"

"I do." She raced to the back, pulling out the

rest of the treats from The Fruit and Nut Tree. Then she gathered the taffy. "I'm wearing the last gift." She dug into her purse and pulled out the notes.

"Okay. So what does all this tell us?"

"Well, these are all my favorite things," she said. "And this is my favorite holiday, so I know it's someone who knows me." She pulled out all the notes and laid them out on the counter. "But nothing in these notes tell me anything."

"The way they are written doesn't say anything?" Kendra lifted one of the cards.

"Not really. I mean, they aren't anything special. Just personal to me."

Kendra nodded. "They aren't romantic and look at this." She tapped the back of the cards. "These were printed in Germany."

Shelly's heart dropped to the pit of her stomach. Her pulse increased. "According to my father, Axel and his team were in Germany, which covers Maverick, Jet, and a few others." She focused her attention on the taffy. The candy came from the one of the local chain stores. "This is from the airport shop."

Kendra snagged the last of the fruit snacks. "This is from the airport as well."

"That isn't helping me much," Shelly said as she

examined the box the jewelry came in. A receipt fell from the bottom. She held it between her thumb and forefinger. "Oh, my God."

"What is it?"

"This was bought the day before Axel was deployed. He called asking if I'd see him before he left. He asked me to meet him at the market. I refused." She stared at the signature on the receipt. "Axel bought this for me. He's my secret admirer."

"He's been playing a fucked-up game," Kendra said.

Shelly swiped at her face. "Not if you knew him like I do." Five thirty couldn't come fast enough.

At exactly five, Shelly locked the floral shop doors. She spent the next fifteen minutes changing her shirt from a boring black T-shirt to a red sleeveless blouse and her favorite jean mini skirt. After fixing her hair and makeup, she stood in front of the mirror in her office and let out a long breath.

This was the moment of truth.

She tossed her purse over her shoulder and made her way to the pier. With every step, her heart pounded a little heavier in her chest. She fiddled with the new necklace dangling between her breasts. It had to have been hard for Axel to put together these little surprises considering his past.

A tinge of guilt floated across her body. She put so much energy into one holiday instead of the man who made her happy.

When she got to the pier, she could see him leaning against the railing at the other end. He stared out at the ocean with his back to the shore.

She slowed her pace and gathered her thoughts, although she had no idea what she'd say. "Hey."

He turned. "Hey, yourself."

The moon and the stars danced over the ripples of the dark water. The sweet sound of a violin rang out across the night air, and the soft sounds of romantic chatter from the restaurant filled the evening.

But all that mattered was this moment.

And the man standing in front of her.

"What happened to your secret admirer?" he asked.

"I know it's you." She folded her arms across her chest.

"I see," he said.

"Why put yourself through doing this, especially after you told me the truth?"

"For two reasons." He held up two fingers. "The first being I needed to see how it felt to do the whole Valentine's Day thing and the second being I wasn't completely sure I could tell you the truth about my parents."

"But you did tell me."

He nodded.

"And how did it feel?" she asked, holding her breath. Not that his answer mattered at this point. If he was willing to give them a second chance, she'd take it, with or without the promise of Valentine's Day or anniversaries.

"To be honest, really weird." He closed the gap. "At first I didn't like it. All it did was remind me of who my parents were. Then, after watching your response with the gifts, I started to realize that I could change my narrative, if I worked at it and if I had a little help from someone who I loved, and she loved me back." He took her chin between his thumb and forefinger. "I love you, Shelly. I'll do whatever it takes to win your heart back. And that includes going all out on Valentine's Day." Gently, he pressed his lips over hers in a tender kiss. "Come with me," he whispered.

"Where?"

"My surprise." He took her by the hand and led her down the docks.

As they walked in silence, she glanced at all the magnificent yachts. "Do you remember the week we went on the cruise for my birthday? That was amazing."

"It was," he said. "And I know you can't just take off for a week right now, but this baby is ours for the next two weeks." He pointed to an eighty-foot yacht named: *Happy Right Now*. On the back deck stood a waiter and a bartender next to a table decked out in roses. "I feel really guilty because I had to buy those flowers from your competitor."

"Yeah, next time, don't do that."

He stopped just shy of the walkway and pulled her close. "So, you forgive me for being an asshole?"

"Can you forgive me for moving out and all the horrible things—"

He pressed his finger on her lips. "Nothing to forgive."

"I love you, Axel. It's always been you."

The End

GLASSE AND STEELE BY JEN TALTY

GLASSE AND STEELE

A Sports Short Story

USA Today Bestselling Author
JEN TALTY

*A big thank you to Chelle Olson for making me laugh so hard
I cry. A especially for helping me with this short story. It
would not have come out half as good without your guidance!*

$\mathcal{V}$eronica Steele folded her arms across her chest as she stepped out of the comfort of her warm hotel and into the cold night. The frigid air clung to her skin like a wet tongue on a frozen metal pole. Her long, blond strands blew in front of her face. She flipped her head in hopes of removing the clump of hair covering her eyes. Her father had warned her that the temperatures in Pittsburgh in the middle of fall were nothing like the month of November in Dallas. She shivered as she pulled open the door to the local pub that the kid behind the hotel lobby desk had recommended.

He'd also suggested that she change her clothes.

Well, that wasn't going to happen thanks to the airline. Two more things her father had told her not to do.

First: Don't check your bag. It's not worth it when they lose it.

Second: If you must check your bag, always keep a coat with you.

Now, she was stuck with a three-quarter-sleeve Dallas Cowboys t-shirt, a jean skirt that barely came to the top of her knees, and a pair of flip-flops. At least, it wasn't snowing.

"Are you fucking kidding me?" A man at the far end of the bar tossed a napkin on the counter. "That is the worst play call ever. Does the coach not read the stats reports on the other team?"

Veronica scanned the restaurant and frowned. Only one seat left, and that was at the bar next to the napkin thrower.

"No. No. No. Goddamn it," the man at the bar said. "Why doesn't our quarterback at least *try* to scramble? Dumbass."

"Maybe if your coach played the second-string quarterback, you wouldn't get sacked so much." Veronica plopped herself onto the barstool. She should try to keep her mouth closed, but sitting in a bar during a football game next to a vocal fan of the opposing team was an opportunity she couldn't pass up. Besides, a beer, a good sandwich, and a heated conversation over the football game might make tonight salvageable. "He's faster, stronger, and has so much more potential. Not to mention, he's willing to take risks. Your number one is predictable and has lost his touch."

"But our backup is a hothead, and Coach can't control him. So, until he learns to take some direction, he's going to stay second string." The man sitting next to her gave her the once-over. He arched his brow. "You've got some balls coming in here wearing that shirt and spouting insults at the home team." He reached out his hand. "My name's Marshall. If Dallas pulls out this win, I'll help you sneak out the back."

"I'm Veronica. And, for the record, Dallas *will* win." She took the handsome stranger's hand in a firm grip. "We might be the underdog this year, but your offensive line can't shut down our defense. And your quarterback can't scramble, much less connect with a receiver. He has no confidence, and he needs to be taken out. I guarantee that if you put in the backup, it will light a fire under the rest of the players."

Marshall held up his beer mug. "I wish I could say you were wrong. Can I buy you a drink?"

"I won't say no to a free Corona." She swiveled in her chair and did her best to act as if she weren't checking out the super-sexy man wearing a white, button-down dress shirt with his tie completely undone, and his sports coat hanging on the back of his chair. A dark five o'clock shadow dotted his face. He had jet-black, slightly wavy hair that kissed the top of his collar. It looked a little unruly, but at the same time, sexy, as if he'd walked right off the pages of a men's fashion magazine. But what nearly knocked Veronica off the barstool were his dark blue eyes that held her spellbound. They were as vibrant as the Mediterranean Sea and as captivating as a car accident you couldn't look away from. "And for the record, the airline lost my luggage. Otherwise, I'd be wearing a bulky sweatshirt, which next time I'll remember take on the plane."

"That's always a good idea," Marshall said.

The bartender set a fresh beer on the counter along with a menu.

"Oh, I know what I want," she said as she shoved her lime into the glass bottle. "One of those weird sandwiches Pittsburgh is famous for. You know, the ones with French fries, coleslaw, cheese, and tomatoes."

Both the bartender and Marshall laughed.

"Sweetheart, that's the Almost Famous, and you can only get them at a Primanti Brothers restaurant," Marshall said. "There is one about three miles away, and they will have the game on."

That would require her to take a Lyft, and besides being starving, she didn't want to go out in the cold again until she had to. "I'll just take a cheeseburger with lettuce and tomatoes, a side of fries, and a side of coleslaw."

"I can do that," the bartender said with a big grin. "But it will cost extra since you're a Dallas fan."

"Just put it on my tab." Marshall clinked his beer against hers.

"No way. I'll take a drink, but not a meal. I'm not here to meet anyone. I just want to watch the game, stuff my face, and get a little buzzed." She handed the bartender her credit card.

"Understood," Marshall said. "But how about we make this interesting? If the Dallas win, I'll pick up the tab. But if the Steelers wins, it's your treat."

"Hey, Marshall, look at this." The bartender held up the piece of plastic she'd given him. "The last name is Steele, and yours is Glasse. Kind of ironic when you consider we are in the city of steel and glass."

"That's amusing," Marshall said, pointing to the television as everyone in the bar let out a collective gasp. "Your team scored."

"And we're about to go up by one since they will do a fake and go for the two-point conversion."

"This early in the game? That's unlikely." Marshall tipped his beer to his lips and stared at the screen above the bar. "Holy shit."

"I told you."

"How did you know?" He set his beer on the counter.

Discussing football typically gave her a thrill, but with him staring at her with unblinking eyes, it only made her nervous. It reminded her of what she faced in the morning and what it meant for her career. "When your coach was the offensive coordinator for the Dolphins—"

"He was fired for making rash decisions," Marshall said.

"He was traded three times as a player for taking unnecessary risks."

"You're making my point for me." Marshall waved his beer in the air. "That's the same reason he won't put in our second string. It's one thing to take a calculated risk—one that pays off more often than not. Or a Hail Mary at the end of a game. But when his decisions cause more losses than wins, well…those risks aren't worth it."

"The problem now is that your coach is gun-shy, and everyone in the league knows it. And they are going to exploit it. But if he occasionally does the unexpected and opens his eyes to his weak spots, he'll change the trajectory of the season."

"You know what? I think you might be right."

"I know I'm right." And that was exactly the attitude Veronica needed tomorrow. She sipped her beer and waited patiently for her food. Maybe, after the interview, she could find an actual Primanti sandwich. Hell, if she got the job and moved to this cold tundra, she could have one whenever she wanted.

That was if she liked the Almost Famous sandwich.

She glanced at Marshall. If the food was anything like the view, she was going to love it here.

2

*M*arshall watched the sexy lady pile French fries and a dollop of coleslaw onto her cheeseburger as she tried to build her own Primanti sandwich.

"This looks disgusting but smells amazing." Veronica lifted half the sandwich and brought it to her mouth. A large clump of coleslaw and a glob of mayo landed on the plate.

He laughed. "And it's messy."

"My taste buds just went crazy." She wiped a finger across her mouth. "Something tells me I'm not even getting this one close."

"I can tell you from experience, you can't create an original Primanti Sandwich. There is nothing like it anywhere."

"I feel that way about my grandmother's

chicken-fried steak. No one makes it better than her. I've tried a hundred different places, and it's never anywhere near as good."

He pushed his empty plate to the side and wiped off his hands. "Six minutes is a lot of time at the end of a game."

"You'd have to score a touchdown and a field goal to win." Veronica dunked a lime into her beer and brought the longneck to her plump lips. She had a petite frame, at maybe five foot four, but it was her spunky personality that had him re-thinking his plans for the rest of the evening.

"Many teams have come back from a more significant deficit with about the same amount of time." For the last couple of hours, Marshall had discussed the finer points of football with a woman who he couldn't stop staring at—and he'd tried, more than once. He'd come to the bar to drink, eat, and watch the game with a room full of strangers so he didn't have to be alone, but he hadn't expected to find a sassy blonde who was more entertaining than the game.

His ex-girlfriend would have a field day with that concept since one of the reasons she'd dumped his sorry ass was because he valued sports more than her. Or so she'd said. He rubbed the side of his shoulder where his electric razor had landed when she tossed it at him the day she'd kicked him out.

But sports, specifically football, was his job, and over the last couple of hours, he'd discovered what he needed to tweak in his algorithm for his report tomorrow—all thanks to Veronica. Hopefully, the organization would take his thoughts—*hers*, actually —seriously.

Everyone in the bar shouted angrily at the television when Pittsburgh fumbled the ball. Not only did Dallas recover it, they also ran it all the way in for a touchdown.

"Looks like dinner is on me." He tapped his finger on the counter. "Close me out," he said to the bartender.

"You don't have to do that," Veronica said as she rested her warm hand on his biceps.

That put his libido into overdrive.

"I insist." He nodded at the bartender. "It's snowing outside. Do you need a ride?"

She lowered her chin and raised a brow. "What kind of girl do you think I am?"

He bit back a laugh. "I didn't mean to imply anything other than it's freezing outside, and you don't have a coat or proper shoes. I just want to make sure you get home in one piece."

A sweet smile spread across her face. Her

almond-colored eyes twinkled with mischief. "That's kind of you, but I'm staying at the hotel right around the corner."

"Why don't you at least let me give you my coat and walk you to the lobby."

"With the way everyone here is eyeing me, I'll take you up on that offer." She tipped her beer. "But I don't want to give you the wrong impression. I'm not inviting you up to my room. I've got a busy day tomorrow."

Boldly, he took her hand in his and pressed his lips against her soft skin. "My mother did raise me to be a gentleman. I wouldn't expect to be invited up, but I *would* like your phone number. Maybe next time you're in town, I can buy you a real Primanti Brothers sandwich."

"I'd like that. If all goes as planned, I'll be back in a couple of weeks for an extended stay."

"Now that sounds promising." He hopped off the bar stool. Snagging his sports coat, he draped it over her shoulders. "Shall we go brave the cold?" Had it not been so late, he might have offered to buy another round. He found himself enjoying the timbre of her voice, and her smile made his heart beat a little faster. He hadn't gone on a single date since his break-up. It had less to do with being heartbroken—which he wasn't—and more to do with how busy he'd been at work and the fact that it was football season.

"Do you ever get used to the cold?" Veronica tugged his suit coat tighter around her body. Wet snow melted the moment it landed on her tanned skin.

He looped his arm around her waist and guided her down the street. "I don't mind the cold or the snow, but I don't like it when it's more rain than snow."

"That doesn't answer my question." Her shoes made a smacking noise with every step she took.

"I've lived in Pittsburgh my entire life; I don't know any other climate."

The lobby doors swung open, carrying a rush of warm air. He stepped inside, wishing he were the type of man who would push for an invitation upstairs. "How long are you in town this time? I could take you for a real sandwich tomorrow evening."

"That's kind of you, but my flight leaves at seven p.m." She pulled her cell out of her back pocket and handed it to him. "Call yourself. That way, you'll have my number, and I'll have yours. If tomorrow goes the way I want it to, I'll be spending a lot more time in this snowy, wintery wonderland."

"I had a shit day at work today, but meeting you

tonight made up for it in spades. You're a lot of fun."

"I had a great time, too." She turned and pressed the elevator button. "What the hell," she muttered as she curled her fingers around his biceps and yanked him into the elevator with her. "You want to come upstairs, right?"

He gripped her hips, pressing her back against the mirrored wall. He searched her face for a reason he shouldn't go to her room, but she stared at him while biting her lower lip. Talk about a sexy expression; one he found nearly impossible to turn down. "Of course, I do. But—"

She hushed him by holding onto his shoulders, lifting to her tiptoes, and slipping her tongue into his mouth, swirling it around in a dance that made him dizzy. "I don't want you to think I'm a floozy."

"I don't want you to believe I'm a player."

She laughed. "You don't have the right kind of moves."

He opened his mouth, but the elevator dinged. He followed her down the hallway, watching her hips sway back and forth as she walked. Her calf muscles flexed, and he found himself wanting to bend over and kiss them. Who was he kidding? He wanted to kiss every inch of her body. Run his tongue over every soft mound and dive into every crevice.

"I must have some moves, or I wouldn't be stepping into your hotel room."

She slammed the door shut behind them. Her fingers toyed with the hem of her shirt. A sultry smile slowly stretched from one cheek to the other.

Quickly, he yanked his tie over his head and tossed it across the room. His chest heaved. It became difficult to fill his lungs when she exposed the white, lacy bra that lifted her full breasts, pushing them together in an erotic picture that made him drunk with desire.

Thank God he'd been carrying around a condom in his wallet. He dug into his pocket and tossed it on the nightstand before removing his belt.

"I don't do things like this." Veronica kicked off her flip-flops and hooked her thumbs on the waistband of her jean skirt. "I recently broke up with my boyfriend of two years. He's the reason I'm looking for a change." She rolled the denim over her hips.

Marshall stood by the edge of the bed, staring. Her sun-kissed skin shimmered under the light of the moon that filtered in through the window. He licked his lips.

"I'm totally over him, but it's been a while." She

dropped her hands to her sides. "Wow. I sound pathetic."

"Not even close. I like listening to you talk, and I want to know whatever you want to tell me." Swiftly, he unbuttoned his shirt and let it fall to his feet. "Besides, I understand. My ex and I ended our relationship months ago. But I've been so busy with work, I barely have five minutes to myself. Going out tonight was a treat."

"Looks like you get a treat *and* dessert." She did a little curtsy. Closing the gap between them, she reached behind her back and unhooked her bra.

He swallowed.

Hard.

It had been months since he'd had sex. And years since he'd had sex with anyone other than his ex. Not that he was worried he'd forgotten how. That would be absurd. But he *was* concerned for his heart because, for the first time in a long while, he found himself wanting to get to know a woman.

Yanking his pants off, he pushed all the lovey-dovey thoughts out of his mind. She didn't even live in Pittsburgh, and it would be a long time before he'd be able to work regular hours again. "You're incredibly beautiful."

"I bet you say that to all the—"

"You're the only lady that matters right now."

He pulled her to his bare chest and crashed landed his mouth on hers, swirling his tongue, tasting her sweet nectar. Her hair smelled like an orchard, and her supple skin tempted his fingertips. Lifting her off the floor, he gently placed her on the bed and removed her scant panties along with the rest of his clothes.

He tangled himself with her, kissing every inch of her tight body. He did his best to keep the pace of his lovemaking tender and slow, but she had a raw animal instinct that pushed him over the edge.

With every tender stroke of her hand, his breath caught in his throat. Their bodies melded together as though they were old lovers reunited after a long separation.

The room filled with the sounds of her soft moans and his deep, throaty growls. They collided together, making intense music that shocked his system. His body beaded with perspiration as he allowed himself to be lost in their passion. He hadn't been prepared for such deep desire, and now that he'd experienced it, he wasn't sure he could ever let it go. Or Veronica.

But did he even have a choice?

Her body quivered as she called out his name, bringing his climax to the surface. Long moments passed as they caught their breath.

He collapsed on the bed, closing his eyes and pulling her close. He had no desire to leave her side, but he knew that his time with her was about to come to an abrupt end.

She patted his chest and glanced up at him with a sexy smile. "Are you ready for me to stroke your ego?"

"Sweetheart, you've already sent my ego to new heights, thank you very much."

3

*V*eronica stretched out her arm and blinked open her eyes. "Where are you going?" She propped her head on her hand and watched Marshall hike his slacks over his tight ass.

"It's almost six, and I've got to be to work by seven."

She dropped her head back to the pillow. "That's when I've got to get up."

"So, why don't you go back to sleep?" He sat on the edge of the bed and pulled her into his arms. "I'm not a fan of one-night stands, and I like you, but this is my busy time of year with work."

"You don't have to explain anything to me. I understand. And things in my life are crazy right now, too."

Cupping her cheeks, he held her gaze for a long

moment. "You're a special woman, Veronica, and I hope I get to be with you again soon."

"The feeling is mutual." Letting the sheet drop to her waist, she wrapped her arms around him and kissed him with her breasts shamelessly pressed against his bare chest.

He groaned. "I really have to go. I have a report due, and my boss is a pain in the ass." He slipped from the bed and finished dressing. "Good luck with your presentation today."

"Thanks." She had no idea why she hadn't told him about the job interview, other than maybe she didn't want to jinx it. This position was the opportunity of a lifetime, and if she were being honest with herself, she'd be devastated if she didn't get it. "Can you hand me my phone before you leave?"

"Sure thing." He set the cell on the pillow. "It would probably be really weird if I asked to take your picture right now."

"Weirdly flattering, but as long as I'm totally covered, and it's for your eyes only, go right ahead."

He smiled like a teenage boy who had seen a boob for the very first time. He held up his cell, and she did her best not to giggle like a schoolgirl as he took the picture.

"I'll talk to you later." He winked right before closing the door.

No way in hell would she be able to go back to sleep for half an hour, so she found the customer service number for the airline.

"Hello. This is Veronica Steele. My luggage went missing on my flight to Pittsburgh. I've got a claim number. It's 89964219."

"One moment please," a young man said.

The sound of clicking came over the line.

"Oh. Yes. We found the bag."

"Thank God. Yesterday, I was told it would be delivered to my hotel. I'm in a bit of a crunch for time because I have a job interview this morning."

"Ms. Steele. I'm so sorry, but your bag is in Tulsa. We can have it sent to Baltimore, but it won't make it to Pennsylvania until eleven."

"That doesn't do me any good. And I fly back to Dallas tonight."

"We can have it sent there," the man said. "And I'm authorized to issue you a two-hundred-dollar voucher to help cover any costs for your inconvenience. I can have that sent to your billing address."

She let out a long sigh. "Thanks. I appreciate it. Please just send the bag back to Dallas. I can pick it up at the airport when I arrive."

"It will be with customer service in baggage claim. Is there anything else I can do for you?"

"No." She tapped the screen and tossed the cell onto the mattress. How in the hell had her luggage ended up in Tulsa? Well, at least they had found it, and they were giving her money. That was something.

But that didn't help her with her interview or the fact that all she had to wear was her outfit from last night. Besides the clothing being inappropriate for any professional setting, wearing a Dallas Cowboys shirt to a potential job with the Pittsburgh Steelers would be the kiss of death.

But what choice did she have?

"What's up?" Marshall peeked his head into his boss's office.

Marshall had been working for the Steelers organization for the last five years. Last month, he'd recently been promoted to lead statistician in charge of the entire data analytics department. He had four people working under him, and currently had one open position on his team.

"Interesting report on last night's game," Tucker said.

"I ended up watching the game with a Dallas fan, and she had some excellent insight. My team will be checking the stats this afternoon. We'll have a completed report to send the coach before dinner." Hopefully, the information would help the coach see the areas where the benefits of risk-taking far outweighed doing things the so-called standard way. Using data analytics this way in sports might be a relatively new concept, but the numbers didn't lie.

"That's great, and in part why I wanted to talk with you." Tucker waved his hand in front of the empty chair next to his desk. "Sunday's game-day report is incomplete."

Marshall didn't have time to explain to his boss for the third time why they weren't finished, but he'd have to suck it up and take a seat. "My team is still looking at all the data regarding the two big upsets. We had to rewrite an algorithm because of it, and I'm taking some of the things I learned from the Dallas fan last night and applying them to past games. We've found a pattern, but I need a little more time. I'm also double-checking everything myself, which is why I'm so glad you're spearheading all the interviews today."

Tucker shook his head. "Not only do I want you to handle the interviews, but I also want you to give all the potentials a tour and grant them access to some of the data to see what their opinions are."

Marshall stiffened his spine. "We agreed you'd do the initial interviews and narrow it down to a couple of candidates, and then I'd give those some demo data to see what they came up with. Why are we changing the process?"

"The data team wouldn't exist had you not talked me into bringing it mostly in-house, and the powers that be are impressed. However, the last person we hired turned out to be less than a good fit, and I believe that's because I did the interviews."

"No. It's because he lied about his qualifications." Marshall pinched the bridge of his nose. This was not how he wanted to spend his day.

"This team is your baby. There are five scheduled today." Tucker pushed a folder across his desk. "They are coming in a half hour apart, starting at eight thirty."

"That's crazy, and it's going to take up my entire day. My team is depending on me to finish the new algorithm."

"Can't they do that?" Tucker asked with an all-knowing, arched brow.

"I suppose." Of course, they could, but that wasn't the point. Marshall glanced at his Apple watch. He had forty-five minutes to finish the algorithm before the first interview. He should be able to do it, but he'd have to pull one of his team members off their project to work with him in case time ran out. "I better get to work." Marshall stood and tucked the folder under his arm.

"You've got the conference room for the day. I've informed the coach that your report might be delayed another twenty-four hours. He's okay with it but will take any partial data you feel comfortable giving him."

Marshall felt bewildered that Tucker hadn't led with that information, but it made no difference. "I'll make sure he gets something by lunch." With that, Marshall left his boss's office and headed to his own that he shared with his team.

It was going to be one hell of a long day.

He tapped the picture icon on his phone and smiled. At least he had the memory of last night to keep him from going crazy.

4

*V*eronica gripped the door handle and sucked in a deep breath as she stepped into the business office of the Pittsburgh Steelers.

The receptionist's jaw dropped. She quickly snapped it shut. "How may I help you?"

"I'm Veronica Steele. I have an interview today."

The receptionist blinked, her mouth still gaping open. "An interview? Here?"

"Yes. With Mr. Winston."

"Lisa," a familiar man's voice echoed from down the hall. "There has been a change of plans. I want you to send all interviewees to my office, not the conference—" Marshall stopped mid-step and mid-sentence about ten feet away. "Veronica? What are you doing here?"

She opened her mouth, but only a grunt escaped her lips. She cleared her throat. "Me? What are *you* doing here?"

"I work here," he said.

"You two know each other?" the receptionist chimed in with a grin. "Well, that's interesting, because she's your first applicant."

"You're not Tucker Winston." Veronica reached for her hair and frowned. This is why she never wore it up. Quickly, she shoved her hands into her pockets. "I was supposed to meet with Mr. Winston." This couldn't be good. Her heart hammered in her chest, and her cheeks flushed.

"Since I run the data team, my boss asked me to do all the interviews." Marshall waved his hand. "Why don't we start with a quick tour of the office?"

She nodded as if she were a bobblehead. If she hadn't had that third Corona last night, she wouldn't have thrown caution to the wind and flung herself at Marshall. Had she not slept with him, this wouldn't be so awkward.

And this position was more than her dream job.

It represented a change in her life that she should have made a year ago.

"Can I ask you a crazy question?" she whispered as they walked down an empty hallway.

"I doubt it will be crazy, but shoot."

"You didn't know I was your first interview this morning?" She clenched her fists. Being played would be worse than having to walk away from a job because of her lousy choices.

"I found out less than an hour ago that Tucker wanted me to run the interviews today. I haven't even looked at any of the candidates. I was too busy using some of the information you unwittingly gave me as we watched the game last night to tweak a new algorithm. So, trust me, I'm as shocked as you." He glanced over his shoulder. His broad smile only made her pulse increase. "Bold choice in clothing."

She narrowed her eyes.

He had the nerve to laugh. "Don't worry about it. We're pretty relaxed around here."

"Right. Because your designer suit and tie scream 'casual.'"

"Yeah, well, according to my team, I'm uptight." He rested his hand on her back and nudged her toward an open door. "You didn't tell me your business meeting was a job interview."

"I'm weird about things like that."

"It does put me in a sticky predicament."

Her stomach lurched. She glanced up at him. "Maybe I should pull my application."

"No. I don't want you to do that." He rubbed the back of his neck. "But because of last night, I don't feel as if I should be the one with the final say on who gets hired."

"I'm not comfortable having this conversation with you."

"I have an idea. Since my boss changed the hiring process on me last minute, I'm going to let my team make the final decision." He held up his hand, wiggling his fingers. "I've got five interviews today, and my boss didn't spread them out. The next one will be here in a half hour, and I've been trying to figure out how to do this. But now I know."

"Please don't put me at an unfair advantage by telling me this strategy," she said. "I need to go. This is a bad idea."

"By taking myself out of the hiring equation, it's a great idea." He curled his fingers around her biceps. "Most people would have called to reschedule because of lost luggage. But not you. Nope. You sucked up your pride and showed up wearing a Dallas Cowboys shirt of all things. That tells me you want this job, and you deserve your shot, regardless of what happened between us."

"But—and this is just a hypothetical—what if I get the job? What happens then? Because—"

"We'll cross that bridge if we get there. Now, let's jump right in and meet the team."

5

"*I* want to thank everyone for staying today. I know it's been the hardest on those who were here first, and I know some of you have other places you need to be this afternoon."

Veronica crossed her arms over her chest and kept her gaze on her flip-flops instead of Marshall. It took a lot to make her uncomfortable in her own skin, but sitting in a room with four other professionally dressed people applying for the same job made her skin feel as though she'd been rolling around on sandpaper.

That said, she had to admit that she'd had a lot of fun playing around with Marshall's algorithms and data analysis. Talk about impressive. Wow. The man had to be one of the smartest people she'd ever come across in this business. To work with him would be a dream come true. She wanted this job even more now. So much so, that she'd gladly give up any personal relationship, sexual or otherwise, with Marshall if it meant she would be offered the position.

"Each of you brings something unique and different to the organization, and I'm honestly impressed with all of you. This is not going to be an easy decision."

Thank God he wasn't going to announce who'd gotten the position in front of everyone. That would have sucked. Veronica sat up taller and rested her hands in her lap. She'd spent a little time problem solving with each of the other candidates, and they were all smart and qualified. Any of them could be offered the job.

"I'm hoping we will have an answer in the next hour. As we discussed, the new hire can start immediately," Marshall said. "Thank you all for coming in, and I'll be in touch."

The other four candidates jumped out of their seats and rushed toward Marshall and the rest of his team. They all stretched out their hands and offered praise and thanks, along with a dozen reasons why they were the best for the job. Veronica chose to take a more laid-back approach and waited for things to calm down before thanking each member of Marshall's team individually and then quietly making her way toward the elevators.

"Thanks for staying," Marshall said as he stepped between her and the cab doors. "I should have payroll take your information for the day. You might as well have handled half of those interviews."

She tried to hide her smile, but it proved impossible. "Sadly, I get off on running numbers."

"I'll remember that next time I'm alone with you in the bedroom," he whispered.

Heat rose from the bottom of her feet to the top of her head. "That's not how—never mind." She pressed the elevator button. "I've got a flight to catch. When will you be making the phone calls?"

"Before you board."

She had so much she wanted to say, but the other candidates stood only a couple of feet away as they too waited for the elevator. "It was a pleasure meeting you."

He leaned in a little too close. "I want to kiss you so bad right now."

Her cheeks flushed, but she ignored his statement. "I look forward to hearing from you." She slipped into the elevator, stepping into the corner as her counterparts stood in front of her. She nodded, giving Marshall an all-knowing smile.

No matter what happened, he'd be a memory she'd take to her grave.

He'd be the one that got away.

The next hour went by in a haze. Veronica stood in the security line at the airport. For the most part, she'd managed to shut her mind down, keeping thoughts of a naked Marshall from her mind's eye, along with the excitement of the data team he'd put together. His concepts were truly cutting edge and would change the way all industries analyzed the data they collected.

Marshall wasn't an average numbers geek. He was pure genius, and Veronica wanted on his team...

And in his bed.

But she couldn't have either.

"Veronica," a male voice called out.

She took a step toward the TSA agent and glanced over her shoulder. She dropped her cell, her boarding pass, and her driver's license to the floor. "Marshall?"

He bent over and picked up her belongings before tugging her to the side. He lifted a large plastic bag. "I brought dinner."

"What?" She watched two people pass through security.

"Don't go back to Dallas. Have dinner with me."

The sudden ringing in her ears intensified. "I need to go home, and you have phone calls to make."

"I've made all but one." He looped his arm around her waist and tugged her away from the security line.

She dug in her heels. "I've got a plane to catch, and you're making me late."

"We need to talk about a couple of things," he said, dropping his hands to his sides—the large, plastic bag bouncing against his thigh. "I thought we could do it over dinner."

She focused on the words written across the plastic.

PRIMANTI BROS.

"Is that one of those sandwiches?" Why did he have to be the kind of guy that thought about other people? Why couldn't he have just let her get on the plane and called her tomorrow with the sad news that he'd hired someone else? Instead, he had to show up with food in hand to deliver the bad news personally.

"I thought we could celebrate."

Her heart skipped a beat and then increased to a dangerous level. "What do we have to celebrate?"

"The fact that my team voted unanimously that they want you for the job."

"Your team, or you?" God, how she wished she hadn't slept with him. If she hadn't, she might be able to believe that he had nothing to do with their decision.

"My team. I didn't even make a recommendation. But I do agree with them. You are the best person for the job. Though that's not the reason I raced down here with two sandwiches in hand."

She swallowed her breath.

"Is there anything you have to get back to Dallas for tonight?"

She nodded. "My suitcase is there."

"There is a mall a few miles from my apartment. We can stop and get you essentials for the next few nights. Then, this weekend, I'll go to Dallas with you to get whatever you need. After, we can come back here and look for a place for you to live, although I know there is a unit in my building for rent."

"Can you please slow down?" She took him by the hand and navigated the sea of people waiting to enter security. "I'm exhausted, and I'm not exactly following what you're saying." She might be tired, but she didn't miss his meaning, she just needed a moment to take it all in. "The position is mine if I want it?"

"Yes." He took her chin between his thumb and his forefinger. "And we can explore whatever this is between us."

"Don't the Pittsburgh Steelers have a no-fraternizing rule or some—?"

"Not in the department we work in." Marshall paused to give her a quick but passionate and meaningful kiss. "Are you going to take the job?"

"Yes," she said calmly, only her heart beat so fast, she thought it might burst right out of her chest.

"Are you going to come back to my place and eat these sandwiches with me?"

"Only if we can do it naked."

The End

FINDING JOBE BY JEN TALTY

FINDING JOBE

A Romantic Short Story

by
USA Today Bestselling Author
JEN TALTY

1

---

 aptain Zayden Topher of the United States Navy tipped his head back and downed a shot of the smoothest tequila he'd ever tasted. It had to have cost a pretty penny, but he wasn't paying, so what did he care. He swiped his lips and slammed the glass on the bar. "I'm done." He blinked. The effects of the alcohol hit his brain like a submarine punching through the surface of the ocean.

Fast and hard and with a splash.

Thankfully, he'd been drinking massive amounts of water and had only a couple of beers and two shots over the course of two hours.

He should be fine.

The operative word there was should.

His eye caught the pretty lady sitting at the end

of the bar, alone. She wore the weight of the world in her ocean-colored eyes. She fiddled with the bottom of her martini glass, her gaze fixated on her cell, ignoring her surroundings.

Especially the group of men sitting at the table about ten feet away who obviously wanted the lady to at least turn her head.

"You're such a lightweight," Lieutenant Colonel Karl Rector, a teacher at the Naval War College, said, pulling Zayden back to the current conversation.

"Don't I know it." Zayden and Karl went all the way back to bootcamp. While their career paths had been vastly different, and Karl outranked Zayden, they had remained close friends.

More like brothers.

"Besides, I've got to get up early." Zayden's gaze kept returning to the pretty brunette sipping what appeared to be a lemon drop while staring at her phone as if she were willing it to ring.

"What the hell are you talking about?" Karl slapped him on the back. "Your transport flight isn't scheduled to leave until noon."

"I haven't even packed and the chick who is subleasing my place is coming around ten. I've just got a shit ton of stuff to do and flying in a C-130 hungover is not fun, even if it is a short flight."

"True. So very true." Karl nodded. "I can't believe you took the job as a teacher at the War College, but I'm so excited to be working side by side with you."

"I am too," Zayden admitted. It would be strange to give up captaining his own submarine, but it was time. He was nearly forty, and his wife had left him three years ago, though their marriage partially ended when they buried their son. But he was tired of being underwater half of the year and he wanted a do-over. He loved his job and he still couldn't imagine resigning from the Navy altogether.

However, it was time to put down some roots and maybe give the relationship thing a try. He'd wanted to patch things up with his ex, but she'd up and married a boring banker about three months ago.

However, if she was happy, that's all that mattered.

Something he'd never been able to do in their eight-year marriage.

Zayden took another glance at the woman and wondered who or what etched that kind of sadness on her face.

Karl paid the bill and motioned to the front door.

"Guess I'll see you in about six months." Zayden stepped out of the local pub and onto Thames Street, looking over his shoulder once. A bunch of laughing college students passed him on the sidewalk. Ah, to be young again. "Thanks for everything. I really appreciate the help in finding a place."

"Not sure why you wanted to pay rent now, but hey, whatever floats your boat."

Zayden laughed. "I hate that saying."

"I know. It's why I use it as much as possible around you." Karl pulled him in for a manly bro hug. "My Lyft is here. Take care, man. Be safe out there and don't sink."

"Jesus. You're an asshole."

"That's why you love me."

Zayden watched his longtime friend duck into his ride. The taillights disappeared around the bend. He stuffed his hands in his pockets and stared up at the sky. There were only five men in the bar.

And one woman.

Not a good idea to leave her alone in there.

He turned on his heel and the second he pushed open the door, he knew he'd made the right decision.

Two men, not from the base that he could tell, had made themselves comfortable at the bar and were trying to make small talk with the lady, who obviously wanted to be left alone.

Time to play knight in shining armor.

"Oh, my God. Babe, I'm so sorry." Zayden wedged himself between one of the men and the lady, who had already tried to tell them she didn't want another drink. He looped his arm over the back of her chair and squeezed her shoulder for good measure. "He just wouldn't stop talking and I felt so bad for him. I can't imagine what he's going through. But I put him in a Lyft."

The lady blinked a few times, staring at him with wide, questioning eyes.

"Come on, honey. Don't look at me like that. I'm really sorry. I promise I'll make it up to you."

She tilted her head and smiled. "It's okay, sweetheart. He's lucky to have such a good friend." She patted his hand. "But next time, don't leave me sitting here by myself so long. Not unless you want to sleep alone."

Zayden bit back a laugh. "Now why would I want to do that when I have the most amazing woman ever."

"Keep talking like that and I just might do that thing on the way home you love so much." She winked.

He shifted as his pants became uncomfortable.

The two men slowly slinked away.

"Sorry to have bothered you," one of them mumbled.

"Thank you," she said quietly.

"Not a problem. That was quite the banter."

"I was just playing along. Besides, you missed some of their comments. They certainly don't know how to talk to a lady."

He pulled up a chair. "This is not the right bar for a woman to sit alone and drink."

She let out a short breath and shook her head. "I hate that double standard." She sipped the drink she'd been nursing for the last hour. She had about one gulp left. "You generally don't see women harassing a man drinking his troubles away. I mean, I wouldn't go up to a man and say something like, *hey, how are they hanging? Shall I give them a good squeeze to find out?*"

He covered his mouth with the crook of his elbow as he burst out laughing. "I can't believe you just said that."

"Sorry. But that one guy made a comment about the size of my breasts."

"Jerk," Zayden mumbled. "Would you like me to do something about it?"

She shook her head. "You've done plenty. Thanks."

"I do hear you about men and women. I mean a man *generally* doesn't have to worry about taking a stroll down the street alone at night. But women do and it's getting late, so I'll walk you out when you're ready."

She lifted her phone and stared at the screen.

"Waiting for someone?"

"You sure are nosy." She raised her glass, downing the last drop. "For all I know you're worse than those two idiots over there who had the worse pickup lines and one being how my boobs were the perfect size, as if they'd never seen such a thing before."

Zayden covered his mouth and stifled a laugh.

"What's so funny? Because if you're laughing at my—"

"No. Not at all. Haven't even looked." His gaze shifted.

"Eyes up here, fella."

He cleared his throat. "I was just remembering the line I used to pick up my ex-wife."

"Maybe that's why she's your ex?" the pretty lady said with a cute little smirk and an arched brow.

"No. She married me because she was in love with the idea of being with a sailor. A military wife seemed intriguing to her. She divorced me because I was at sea more than I was at home and according to her, I loved my submarine and the men on it more than I did her."

"Having been an Army brat, I know how tough that life can be. It's not for everyone."

The bartender approached.

"Can I buy you a drink?" Zayden asked.

She glanced at her cell before setting it, screen down, on the bar. "Sure."

"Another whatever that is for the lady and I'll take a Stella and a glass of water."

The bartender nodded.

"May I ask your name?" He should get the hell out of this bar, go back to his new rental, and sleep.

"Only if you tell me the line you used on your ex-wife. I'm dying to know what cheesy thing you came up with that got her to agree to go out with you in the first place."

"What makes you think it was cheesy?"

"You just seem like the kind of guy that carries it well."

He laughed. She wasn't wrong. "I was stationed in Norfolk, Virginia, and I used to see her every morning when I got my coffee and bagel before heading to the base. She was the most beautiful woman I'd ever seen, and I was terrified to even make eye contact."

"Seriously? I mean you came right up to me and put your arm around me."

"That's different."

"What? I'm not pretty?"

"Wow. You're really letting me dig myself a hole here, aren't you?"

The bartender set his beer in front of him none too soon. He took a hearty chug. Not that he'd planned on hitting on this woman. But if he wasn't heading out to sea, he certainly would consider it.

She raised her glass. "Too much booze. Not enough food."

He waved to the bartender. "Can we get a basket of fries?"

"You didn't have to do that," she said.

"I'm starving anyway. Now do you want to hear my story? Because I want to know who I'm breaking bread with."

Finally, she gave him an authentic big smile.

And he damn near fell off his stool. The way her eyes lit up like the sunrays stretching into the waters of the ocean, showing off the wonders below the surface.

He cleared his throat. "Anyway. One morning she wasn't there. I didn't think anything of it. But then a whole week went by, and I started to get worried about her and a million things went through my brain on what could have happened."

"You do know that sounds crazy, right?"

"But she thought it was part of my charm." He nodded. "On the eighth day, she finally showed up and like the big goof that I am, I went right up to her and said, *Are you okay? I haven't seen you in a week and I've been worried about you.*"

"What did she say?"

"She just stood there and stared at me like I had ten heads. A few long awkward minutes passed and I made a bigger ass out of myself and said, *I'm sorry, I'm being deployed tomorrow and I see you here all the time, and for weeks I'd been trying to find creative ways to ask you out and I thought I'd lost my chance.* She burst out laughing as if it was the funniest thing she'd ever heard."

"Wow. Crashed and burned and right before you left for sea."

"That's the worst part. I wasn't shipping out for three more weeks. We went out on our first date and I had to come clean just as she was about to invite me in to give me a really nice send-off."

"At least you were honest."

"Got me laid and a got me a good woman." He clanked his glass against hers. "Too bad I fucked it up. Now she's happily married to someone else."

"At least you're aware of your mistakes and own them. Takes a real man to admit that." She leaned forward. "Or someone who is really good at picking up chicks in bars."

He laughed. "I should tell you that I am shipping out tomorrow." He held up his hands. "But I'm not looking for a one-night stand. Honestly, when I get back from this last tour, I want to settle down for real this time."

She turned her phone over and sighed. "My name is Esme. What's yours?"

"Zayden."

"That's unique."

"So is Esme."

She set her cell down. "It was my grandmother's nickname, and I was born the day she died. My father decided her soul was reborn in me."

"Jesus. You're going to make a grown man cry."

She patted his shoulder. "Are you for real? Because I've never met anyone like you before."

"Trust me. I have my faults as my ex-wife will tell you."

"Do you have kids?"

He swallowed the lump in his throat. "We did." He rarely discussed his son, Sheldon, named after his ex-wife's late father.

"Did?" She grabbed his hand and squeezed. "What does that mean?" Her eyes filled with tears.

He shook his head. "You don't want to hear this. It's totally a downer topic."

"No. I want to know what happened. Please."

Taking in a sharp breath, he exhaled slowly. Who was he to deny a beautiful woman? "Sheldon, that's my son, was born while I was deployed, a fact my ex never let me forget."

"You had no control over your deployments."

He tilted his head. "Not entirely true, but this was a war training exercise, and my son was born three weeks early. Had he waited two weeks, I would have made it." Zayden paused to take a swig of his beer. "I took a year shore duty so I could spend time with my family. When Sheldon was nine months old, we noticed he didn't seem right. He was pale and just seemed tired all the time. My ex-wife took him to the doctor and they brushed it off as common things. I shipped off on my next four-month tour. While was on that submarine, we found out Sheldon had Leukemia."

"Shit. I'm so sorry."

"I came home as soon as I heard, but it wasn't soon enough. My ex hated me for not being there with her when Sheldon had been diagnosed and that it took me two weeks to make it home. She'd been begging me from the second she got pregnant to give up my commission, but being captain of a sub had been my dream." He stiffened his spine, forcing himself to stay strong. He'd had just enough booze to allow the tears to escape. He couldn't have that. Not now. Not tonight. "No matter what the doctors did, they couldn't save Sheldon. He died three months after I returned."

"I'm so very sorry for your loss."

"Thank you." He never knew what to say to people who offered their condolences, but she seemed so genuine he felt the need to take her hand and give it a little squeeze. "I spent three more months at home, but then I was called back to duty. My ex just didn't understand. But it was a year later when I re-enlisted that basically ended our marriage."

"Having a sick child is hard enough on keeping a marriage going. Losing a son either brings you together or tears you apart." A few tears dribbled down her cheeks. She swiped at them before taking a few swallows of her lemon drink.

He considered himself a good judge of character as well as having the ability to read people and she carried the burden of the kind of pain that no parent should have to bear. "You speak as if you know."

"My daughter has leukemia. But that's not what broke up my marriage."

He scooted closer, resting his arm on the back of her chair. "What's your daughter's name?"

"Jillian."

"That's a pretty name."

Esme nodded, holding out her phone. "That's my baby girl. She just turned eight three days ago."

"She's beautiful and she looks just like you."

"She has my eyes, but she has her father's nose." Esme titled her head and smiled as she glided her finger across the image. "Not that we've seen him much in six years. He skipped out as soon as the divorce became final and we don't hear from him often. Except for the occasional check when he decides to pay, which isn't on a regular basis."

"He doesn't come see his daughter?"

"He did once when we first found out, but he can't handle it. Says it's too much and that he doesn't really know her anyway."

"When was she diagnosed?" Zayden's heart broke in a million pieces.

"A few months ago. She's in the hospital right now undergoing treatment. My sister just moved here to give me a hand. She's at the hospital, staying the night, giving me a break." Esme flipped some hair over her shoulder. "This is my first night away from her since she started this round of chemo."

"I know it's hard not to be there, but if you let yourself get run down or worse, you won't be much good to her." He reached across her and tapped her cell. "Is that why you keep looking at your phone?"

"Yeah. I keep waiting for something to happen and for my daughter to beg me to come in or my sister to say she can't handle it. But I know that won't happen. My sister and Jillian have a special bond. It's actually really sweet and I'm lucky to have such an amazing support system with Adeline. That's my much older sister."

He swallowed the emotional lump stuck in his throat. His ex-wife hadn't had the best relationship with her family, nor did she have a ton of friends down in Jacksonville, where he'd moved them shortly after they'd gotten married. "You really need to take short breaks for yourself and if your daughter is good with hanging with your sister for the night, then let it happen." He ran his hand up and down her back. "But you should also take the time to get a good night's sleep because I'm sure you're not getting that on a regular basis." He waved to the bartender for the bill. He'd put Esme in a Lyft, making sure she got home safely, and then he'd get himself back to his new digs.

It was time to call it a night.

"Thank you for coming to my rescue." Esme tossed her purse over her shoulder.

"It's my pleasure, but I'm not letting you leave here alone. Not with those idiots still staring at you. So, we're getting a Lyft together that will do two drop-offs."

"You can do that?"

"If we can't, once you're safe and sound at your place, I'll get into a new Lyft."

"But then you'll know where I live," she said.

"Then we'll go to my place first."

She curled her fingers around his biceps. "Why don't we just go to your place?"

He held her gaze for a long moment. A year ago he wouldn't have thought twice about taking her to bed. After his divorce, his love life had turned into a string of nameless one-night stands and short-lived relationships that left him not only unsatisfied, but allowed him to continue to stay in a dark place.

He didn't want to go back there, and he certainly didn't want to use a woman when she was vulnerable.

Esme deserved better than that.

She dropped her hand and lowered her chin. "I'm sorry."

"No. Don't be." He hopped off his stool and

cupped her cheek. "Trust me. I'd like nothing more than to get to know you better. In more ways than one. But I'm really leaving tomorrow for four months. And please don't take this the wrong way, but I'd feel like I'm taking advantage of a woman who's had a bit much to drink and who is in a bad place."

"Are you for real?"

He chuckled. "Afraid so." He wiped a tear that rolled down her cheek.

"What if I just didn't want to be alone tonight and nothing happened but you were in the same space? Would you be willing to do that?"

He shouldn't even consider her request. It would be crazy. He had too many things he needed to do before he left tomorrow.

But he couldn't leave Esme alone.

"You know, I've done crazier things." He leaned in and kissed her cheek. "Where would you be more comfortable?" And with that question, Zayden sealed his fate.

2

*E*sme had done only one crazy thing in her life and it resulted in both the best and worst thing that had ever happened.

She would never regret having Jillian.

But she did regret marrying her father.

"This is a nice place you have," Zayden said as he kicked off his boots by the front door. "I actually live only about three miles away. It's half a house, but it's nice and will be temporary until I get my land legs and find something to buy."

Esme tossed her keys on the table by the front door. Her New England style Cape Cod was only about a thousand square feet and was nestled between two other similar style homes. She had a single car garage and a small fenced-in backyard that she'd promised to fill with a puppy.

But then Jillian got sick.

"I think my landlord plans on putting this place on the market eventually." She made her way toward the small bar area in the family/dining room and pulled out a bottle of red. She held it up.

He shook his head.

She shrugged. "I wish I could afford it, but I wouldn't have enough for the down payment."

Zayden snatched the wine from her hand.

"Hey. What the hell are you doing?"

"I think you've had enough."

"You have no right to tell me—"

He pressed his fingers over her lips. "I think I do, especially when you asked me to come home and watch over you tonight because you didn't want to be alone. I'm not going to let you get shit-faced and then be so hungover tomorrow that you're no good to your daughter. Trust me on this. You don't want to be that person."

"Why? Because that's the kind of dad you were?" She let out along breath. "Shit. I'm sorry. I don't know what came over me. That was a horrible thing to say." She let him take the wine and put it away. She didn't want to admit it, but he was right. Even though she wasn't too wickedly drunk, she wasn't functioning at full capacity.

"Might be horrible, but it's not completely off base."

"Regardless. I shouldn't have said that just because I'm feeling sorry for myself."

He took her by the hand and led her into the only other room on the first floor, the kitchen. He sat her down at the table and handed her a glass of water before leaning against the counter. "Are you feeling bad because Jillian is in the hospital or because she's fine with your sister?"

"I'm fine with that," she admitted, which was true. Jillian and Adeline, or Addy as everyone called her had such an amazing connection and even if Esme wanted to be jealous, she couldn't because nothing could come between Esme and her daughter. They had a unique relationship. All mother daughter relationships were special, but hers and Jillian's was the kind of bond that couldn't be broken.

No matter what.

Esme polished off her water and stood. "I don't want to get into this, and you don't need to stay with me. Really." She patted his chest. "I'm fine."

He took her hand and kissed the soft sensitive skin of her palm. His hot lips lingered for a lot longer than they should have.

And even after he removed them, the warmth

crawled across her body like lava slowly flowing from a volcano. He had some gray hair popping at the temples and a few deep-set wrinkles at the corners of his ice-blue eyes, showing some years of living. But his body was as solid as a rock. She guessed him to be about ten years older, so maybe forty.

"I don't believe that," he said softly. "You can talk to me. I'll listen."

No one wanted to hear her sob story. Her family was tired of it and didn't want to hear the name Eddy ever again. They thought she should just tell the jerk to fuck off.

But it wasn't that simple.

"Ever since Eddy, that's my ex, showed up to see Jillian, she's been asking when her daddy is going to come back and see her, and it's going to break her little heart when I tell her he's never coming back."

"Never? He said that to you?"

"Pretty much." She stood in the hallway by the stairs. "I don't want to burden you with my problems anymore. You've been amazing. You're a good man, Zayden. I appreciate everything you've done for me tonight."

He inched closer, holding her gaze with his intense stare. Stretching out his arm, he cupped the back of her neck and gently massaged. "You're not burdening me. I'm here because I chose to come. Now what exactly did your ex say to you and what did he say to Jillian?"

Esme couldn't stop the tears if she tried.

He wiped them away with a gentle stroke of his thumb.

How could one man be so tender and kind? Zayden was the type of person that was only written about or portrayed in movies. He was the kind of guy your parents always dreamed you'd bring home, only the moment you thought you found your Prince Charming, they turned into a frog.

It was never the other way around.

"He of course told her that he'd be back as soon as he could, but he told me that he'd left for a reason and just because she was sick, it didn't change that reason."

"Jesus. It sounds like I might want to go find this asshole and knock his lights out."

"You'd have to wait in line. My sister wants to string him from a flagpole by his balls."

"I think I like you sister," Zayden said with a wink. "So, what was the reason?"

Wow. This man didn't give up. She wasn't sure if she loved that about him, or resented it. "Very long story short we'd been broken up when I got pregnant. I pushed hard to get married when he didn't really want to, and he didn't want to be a father. Our relationship was horrible and two years into our shitty marriage, I gave him his walking papers. I only asked he pay me child support. When he doesn't, I threaten him."

"How often has he seen his kid since you've been apart?"

"Once or twice a year and it's always facilitated by me."

"He's no father," Zayden said, shaking his head. "I might have been the worst husband on the planet. I admit to leaving a lot of things up to my ex-wife, but even she'd tell you that when it came down to our son and his illness, once I got home, I was there every step of the way. However, it doesn't make up for all the times I wasn't there."

"I think you're a little too hard on yourself."

He shook his head. "I'm being realistic about my past. But I'm going to tell you something as a person looking at this from the outside. You need to be honest with your little girl. You're not doing her any favors by letting her think her father is going to come back."

"I swore I'd never be the one to taint her view of him. I knew he'd do that on his own."

"Telling her that you don't think he's coming

isn't doing that; it's being honest because you lying to her is only going to make her feel as though the one person who's supposed to support her and love her the most, just betrayed her."

"Wow. When you put it like that, you make it sound so simple."

"Nothing about this situation is easy. And she's going to be hurt and upset." Zayden circled his arms around her waist and pulled her close to his chest. "But you're a good mother and with the support of your sister, Jillian will get through the emotional loss and acceptance of her father's choice. All you can do is move forward and be there for her. At least then, if he decides to move in and out of her life, she'll understand it doesn't have anything to do with her."

"How the hell did you get to be so smart? Are you sure you're really a captain of a submarine and not a shrink?"

He laughed. "I have a master's degree in psychology." He shrugged. "Don't ask. My mother's influence and it's honestly come in handy commanding my own sub." His hands flattened on the small of her back. His fingers lingered dangerously close to the top of her ass.

Resting her hands on his strong, broad shoulders, she tilted her head. "And what does that degree tell you about me being in your arms right now?"

"That I'm in over my head. That I should thank you for a very lovely and unexpected evening and tell you that I'd like to see you when I get back and then walk out that door." His hands roamed under her shirt. She arched into him, letting out a slight gasp at his cool fingertips dancing along her spine as if she were a keyboard and he was a master pianist. "I'm trying to do the right thing and it's not easy. Not only are you beautiful, but you're intelligent, sweet, and funny. You're the kind of woman I'd like to date."

"I have too much baggage."

"I have a whole closet full."

She laughed. "Not what I meant."

He leaned in. His lips hovered over her mouth. The heat radiating from his body coated her skin like a melting marshmallow on top of a piece of chocolate slapped between two graham crackers.

"Tell me to leave."

"No," she whispered.

"Tell me to sleep on the sofa."

"No."

"Then tell me you won't regret this in the morning and that you will at least have dinner with me when I get back."

"Yes."

"To both?"

"Yes," she lied to the latter. She would do her best to make sure she never ran into him again. And if she did, she'd find a million excuses on why they could never be together.

Of course, there was always the possibility that he wouldn't want to see her again, and that would be okay. Her focus needed to be Jillian. This was just a one-night stand, allowing her to get out some pent-up emotions so she could be the best mother ever.

He gently parted her lips with his tongue. He tasted like the salty sea air and she couldn't get enough of him. Her entire body ignited in a fiery ball of passion that only he could put out.

And even then, she doubted he'd ever be able to completely put out the flames.

Something about him got under her skin like no other man she'd ever met before. The way he held her with his hands roaming her body, caressing and molding her muscles with his palms, was tender and sweet, and yet it was also filled with intense desire.

In one swift motion, he lifted her into his arms.

"Whoa," she managed with a ragged breath. "What are you doing?"

"Carrying you upstairs to bed."

"I don't think any man has ever done that with me before."

"Let's make it our thing." He practically ran up the stairs and found her room. He laid her on the bed and ripped off his shirt.

She sat up and traced the heart tattoo on the upper right side of his chest. It was one of three. In the center of the heart were the initials SZT and a date. "Is this your son's birthdate?"

"It is."

"I have something similar." She sat up and took off her shirt, pressing her hand under her left breast, showing off a lily with her and her daughter's names along with her daughter's birth sign.

"That's a cool tattoo." He fingered it, sending goosebumps across her skin.

"Thanks. I take it this has something to do with the Navy?" She palmed the submarine on his other pectoral muscle.

"That's the first and only sub I've ever captained." He took her hand and moved it to the one just below the submarine. "And this one my mother designed. It's of our first family sailboat. Being on the water was always and still is my most favorite place."

"I love the ocean too. So does Jillian." Esme

removed her jeans and lowered her not-so-sexy underpants, revealing her second tattoo, which was quite extensive and not finished yet as it wrapped around her hip.

"Wow." He reached out and palmed her waist. "Is that of the harbor here in Newport?"

She nodded. "It's Jillian's favorite place. Before she got sick, we'd go there all the time and watch the boats come and go. She loved it. So, for the last few weeks, I've been going every couple of days to get this worked on."

"I can tell. It's still red and raw." He glanced over his shoulder. "Is that your bathroom?"

"Yeah. Why?"

"You need to put lotion on that." He tapped her hip before disappearing.

Who the hell was this guy? And why did he have to come into her life when a man was the last thing she needed?

Of course, he was leaving, so what did it matter?

He returned with a handful of goop. He massaged it on her hip, covering her tattoo, and then his hand slipped to her ass, cupping her cheek. He pulled her panties to her ankles and tossed them to the side.

She undid the front clasp of her bra and let it pop open.

He groaned. "I so want to do something completely inappropriate right now."

"You mean how more than a handful is too much?" She cupped herself and smiled.

"Something like that." He hooked his fingers into his pants.

"How about you let me do that." It had been a long time since she'd been with a man and even longer since she'd felt so comfortable that she didn't want to hide under the covers and turn off all the lights.

He ran his hand through her hair as she removed the rest of his clothing.

Shamelessly she did things to him that she'd always been embarrassed to do in the past. Sex had always been something that was a requirement of a relationship. There'd only been a couple of times where she'd felt as though sex might become something different. Something special. Something that she'd fantasized about and something she knew others experienced.

But she had shit luck in men.

Until tonight.

Only he was leaving.

And her daughter needed her undivided attention.

This was a one-night stand.

Plain and simple.

He showed her what her body demanded. Needed. Craved. He found every single erogenous zone she had, and a few she didn't know she had. As soon as her body recovered from one wicked climax, he found a way to give her another.

His own release created such excitement inside her soul, she found herself holding back tears.

She wrapped her arms and legs around him, squeezing tight, burying her face in his neck. She shivered.

"Are you cold?"

"No."

He rolled to the side, pulling the covers over their bodies.

She snuggled in close, resting her head on his chest. Closing her eyes, she let her exhaustion take over her mind, body, and soul. "Thank you for saving me tonight."

He kissed her forehead. "Thank you for giving me something to look forward to' for the next four months."

For a brief second, she held her breath.

Dinner.

"You're welcome," she said softly. No point in disappointing a sailor before he went off to sea. She knew firsthand from her father what it was like and how important it was to know a man or woman had something to come back to.

If only she could have been that woman for him.

3

*Z*ayden shouldn't have been surprised that Esme slipped out without saying goodbye, but at least she left a sweet note.

One that had her full name and address on it, though he wondered if she'd written the note on her personal stationary on purpose, or she just had been in such a hurry to get to the hospital.

He slipped into the back seat of the Lyft. Unfolding the note, he read it one more time.

Dear Zayden,

I will always cherish our night together.

No regrets. Not a single one. And I hope you feel the same way. You're an amazing man and I'm so glad I got to meet you. Though, I will be picking my bars more carefully from now on.

He let out a slight chuckle.

I have no idea what my life will be like in four months when you return. I'm going to think positively and believe that I'll be in a better place and that my daughter will be on the road to a full recovery. I have to believe that. Something I know you understand.

He rubbed his eyes. It never got easier. It just got different.

Trust me when I say I'm not canceling on you already. I'm just saying my focus is Jillian. She will always be first in my life and that will always take precedent over a love life. Feel free to look me up when you return. No matter what the future holds, I will always consider you my knight in shining armor, my personal Prince Charming, and more importantly, a really good friend.

Be safe out there.

Esme.

The vehicle rolled to a stop in front of his duplex. He stepped out onto the pavement. Carefully, he folded the letter and gently placed it in his back pocket.

Yelp. Woof.

He paused, cocking his head. Last night, before he'd gone to the bar, he thought he'd heard a dog barking.

Well, more like whining.

He bent over and glanced under his porch. "Hey there, little fella," he said, staring at a scared, shivering puppy. "Why don't you come on out?" He glanced at his watch. He had two hours before his sublease lady showed up and three hours before he had to be at the base.

Peanut butter.

Dogs loved peanut butter.

He raced inside and snagged a jar. Sitting on the side, he took a big glob on his fingers and held them out. "I won't hurt you."

The puppy sniffed and inched forward, whining. He had no collar and he looked like he hadn't eaten in days. Maybe even weeks.

"It's okay."

The puppy took a quick lap at Zayden's fingers. Then a second. And then finally, the dog attacked the tasty treat until there wasn't a drop left on Zayden's skin.

"There is more where that came from." He put more on his hand, letting the puppy have his fill.

The tiny thing wagged his tail and looked up at Zayden with sad eyes that nearly broke Zayden's heart.

If he had to guess what kind of dog he was looking at, he'd say it was a Golden Retriever.

First thing he'd do when he got stateside would be get a bigger place with a fenced-in yard and then a dog.

"You're cute." He patted the puppy's head. "Where did you come from?" By the looks of him, he figured he'd been living on the streets for a week or so. And he hadn't been neutered yet. Carefully, he reached down and lifted the dog. "You smell."

The puppy tilted his head as if he took offense to the comment.

"You look like my dog Jobe when I was a kid. So that's what I'm going to call you. Any problems with that?" He stepped into his one-bedroom duplex and stared at the pathetic excuse for a place to live. He felt sorry for the young woman who was subleasing the place for the next month or so. "Okay, Jobe. First things first. And that's a bath. Then some food. And then I need to get you to a shelter. One that is going to take good care of you because I've got to leave." Well, shit. All he ever did was leave things and people behind.

He was looking forward to the day he no longer had to let down the people he cared for and still got to keep his job.

One that he loved.

He knew he'd still have to travel. And he knew he could still end up on a ship for a short period of time. He had a specific skill set that the Navy might need in times of crisis.

But he needed to try normalcy.

If he hated it, he could always ask to be transferred again.

However, if he got the chance to sweep Esme off her feet, he'd take it.

He made his way to the only bathroom in the house and set Jobe in the tub, letting him go to town on some more peanut butter. Silly dog didn't even seem to care about the water hitting his feet. Zayden found some body soap and lathered up.

That, Jobe took offense to and tried to run away.

"Oh, no, you don't." He snatched Jobe up and started scrubbing. Eventually, Jobe succumbed and let Zayden get him good and clean. Once he had Jobe all dried off, he set him on the floor and went to finding something substantial for him to eat. "I think I have some hamburger. I hope that will be okay." He glanced down to find the dog chewing on his favorite pair of shoes. "Hey! Stop that!"

Jobe cowered. Peed a little on the floor. Then hid under the table, shaking uncontrollably.

That was very telling.

"I didn't mean to yell," Zayden said, kneeling. "It's okay. We can clean up the mess and you don't ever have to worry. I won't hurt you and I'll find a way to make sure no one else does." He pulled Jobe into his arms and gave him a little scratch behind the ears. "You're a good boy." He was rewarded with a big lick.

He laughed. "Thank God you just had peanut butter." He opened the fridge and found a half-eaten hamburger from the day before. That would have to do. After finding a plate, he ground up the burger, getting rid of all the sides, and set the plate on the floor.

Zayden spent the next hour trying to entertain Jobe, making sure he didn't destroy anything, all while packing. He needed to give himself some time to drop Jobe off at a shelter, only he had no idea where one was located.

Just as he sat down at the kitchen table with a half-asleep puppy at his feet, the doorbell rang.

Jobe jumped to attention and raced to the front door, skidding across the hardwood and slamming his snout into the wall.

Zayden couldn't help it. He laughed. Hard. "Come here, you silly dog." He scooped Jobe up in his arms and pulled open the door. "Oh. Hey. You must be Addy."

"In the flesh," a woman with long blond hair pulled up on the top of her head in a messy bun said. She wore leggings and a tank top. It looked as if she'd just come from a run or something. "And who is this adorable little guy?"

"Well. I just found him an hour ago. But for now, I'm calling him Jobe. I need to find a shelter to drop him off at." He took a quick glance at his watch. "And if I'm going to do that, I'm going to need to leave soon."

"Why don't you let me take care of Jobe?"

"He's not my dog."

"No. I mean, I'll take him to a shelter. Or better yet, I'll find him a good home. I actually know someone who might be in the market."

"Well, I just found him under my porch and I suspect he's been abused since when I yelled at him for chewing on my sneakers, he cowered in a corner as if I were about to beat the crap out of him."

"Oh, that poor little puppy." She stretched out her hands and took him out of Zayden's arms. "Trust me. I know a family who would love to have a dog. They have been talking about adopting for a while now. And if they aren't interested, I'll take him to a shelter. I promise."

"You don't mind?"

"Not at all," Addy said.

"Wonderful. I just need to get a few things from the bedroom, and I'll get you the keys and everything else you will need. The landlord said you don't know how long you will need the place, but just know I'll be back in four months."

"I won't be here that long, but thanks."

Zayden scratched Jobe's head. "Listen. I want to write a little note to go with the dog. Do you mind giving it to whoever ends up with him?"

"Sure. Whatever you want."

"Thanks." Zayden didn't know why he felt so attached to Jobe, but he wanted to know what happened to him and to make sure the little guy was placed in a good home.

He'd never forgive himself if something happened to Jobe.

4

*E*sme glared at her sister. "How could you?"

"What?" Addy shrugged. "You wanted a dog and this guy needed a home."

"You should have asked me before bringing him to the hospital and introducing him to Jillian. You know how she feels about animals. Now she's all attached and if I take him away, I'm the bad guy." She took a sip of her cold coffee. "I'm shocked that they even let him in." Esme waved at her daughter who smiled like she hadn't smiled since she'd been diagnosed with cancer. It warmed Esme's heart to see her baby girl so happy.

But the last thing Esme needed was to deal with a damned dog.

Jobe jumped up on Jillian and licked her face as if they were old friends. Another patient and his nurse strolled by on their outdoor walk in the courtyard. They paused to say hello to the adorable dog that would for sure steal the hearts of everyone.

"How the hell am I going to take care of a dog while Jillian is in here?"

"Seriously? That's what I'm here for." Addy held up her hand. "And it's not like Jillian is going to be in the hospital forever. Having a dog around will be good for her. Look at how happy Jobe makes her. And pets are emotional support. That's why they let me bring him in. They do it all the time because animals boost the spirits of the patients."

"Where the hell did you get this dog anyway? He's not even neutered yet."

"The guy I'm subletting from. He found him this morning under the porch. He thinks he's been abused. He even gave me a grand to make sure the dog gets all his shots and whatnot since I sort of told him I thought I knew someone who wanted a pet."

"Of course you told him that." Esme shook her head. Jillian hadn't looked this excited since she'd won the spelling bee at school. And Esme couldn't take that smile away. "Fine. But you have to deal with taking the dog to the vet and getting him checked out first. And if he's got some strange problem, or has an owner already, you get to tell Jillian."

"Deal," Addy said, jumping up and down like a small child. It was hard to believe that Esme was the younger one. "Can I go tell Jillian we can keep Jobe?"

Esme nodded. She leaned back on the bench and inhaled the fresh Newport salty air.

"Oh. Wait. I forgot something." Addy handed Esme a piece of paper. "Zayden, the guy I sublet from, asked me to give this to whoever took Jobe in."

With a shaky hand, Esme took the envelope. Her heart sank to the pit of her stomach. "Who?"

"Zayden. I know. Odd name. But let me tell you, this guy was hot." Addy fanned herself. "If he hadn't been in such a rush to get out of town, or I hadn't a boyfriend, I would have been throwing myself at him for sure." Addy kicked up her back leg and raced off to be with Jillian and Jobe.

Esme held the envelope in her hands, staring at it as if it might spontaneously combust. This couldn't be happening. No way could she have just adopted a dog that her one-night stand found.

That Zayden found.

She tore open the envelope and tried to swallow

the lump in her throat, but it proved to be impossible.

To whom it may concern,

I know this is unconventional, but I found Jobe just hours before I had to leave for a four-month deployment with the Navy. He was undernourished and I think he might have been abused, though I can't be certain.

He loves peanut butter. And appears to be housebroken, though if you raise your voice at him, he tends to have accidents. He also understands simple commands. Sit, stay, come. So, he's been trained. But again, if you yell or raise your hand too quickly, he will run away and whimper in fear.

I named him Jobe because he reminds me of my childhood dog. And also, I would have kept him had I not had this one last deployment.

So, I ask one huge favor. I know that this is a lot, but I just want to know he's in good hands. Please call me in four months at this number. I'd like the chance to come visit Jobe. I don't want to take him from you; I just want the chance to see how he's grown and thank you for taking him in.

Sincerely,

Zayden Topher

Well, now she knew his last name, something that she hadn't wanted to know because then she could go look him up, if she wanted to.

And she didn't want to.

5

*E*sme leaned back in the Adirondack chair and watched her daughter play fetch with Jobe, who'd grown a lot in the last month. He was a good dog and loved Jillian. He was always at her side. Wherever Jillian went, Jobe could be found.

Esme had tried to keep Jobe to the first floor, keeping the upstairs dog-hair free, but Jobe would manage to break through every barrier just to be able to sleep at the foot of Jillian's bed.

The dog trainer told her that many dogs became attached to children, especially sick children. That they had a kind of sixth sense about it and Jobe took his role as protector pretty darn seriously.

Jillian was getting stronger and her treatments were going well, but only time would tell. The doctors were optimistic and her cancer had been caught early, and Esme held on to that hope.

Only, every time she looked at that damn dog, she thought about Zayden.

And that night.

She tried to tell herself that the dog was the only reason he kept coming into her mind, but she knew better. Zayden had touched her soul and heart in ways no man ever had.

"Hey, sis," Addy's voice rang out in the warm June air.

It had been six weeks since Zayden had shipped out to sea. He'd be back sometime in September. When he returned, he could potentially just show up on her doorstep. She felt so conceited just thinking he would do that. She wasn't that memorable, and four months was a long time.

"Did you get everything all packed up?" Esme would miss her sister dearly, but she couldn't expect Addy to give up her life indefinitely, and while her job allowed her to work from anywhere, she had a life back in Vermont with a boyfriend.

"I did. But you have some explaining to do."

Esme covered her eyes, protecting them from the sun, and turned her head. "About what?"

"About why you're getting letters from Zayden Topher. You acted like you had no idea who that was." Addy dumped an envelope on her lap before plopping down in one of the chairs. "Start talking."

Esme stared at her name printed neatly in blue ink. Her heart beat so fast she couldn't catch her breath. She blinked a few times, unable to focus on anything other than her name. She wanted to tear her gaze away, but she couldn't.

He'd written.

He cared enough to take the time to send her a note.

What did that mean?

Shit. She couldn't bring a man into this mix.

"There's nothing to talk about."

"You are not getting off the hook that easily and I'm not leaving until I get answers." Addy folded her arms.

If there was one thing Esme could count on from her sister, it was that she meant what she said and she'd spend a few more days just to get the dirt.

And Addy always knew when Esme was lying.

She took in a deep breath and let it out slowly. "I met him the night before he shipped out."

"The night I spent at the hospital?"

Esme nodded. "He rescued me from a couple of idiots hitting on me at a bar I had no business being in, and then we just talked. Next thing I knew, he was here and we spent the night together."

"Holy shit. You had a one-night stand with that hottie?"

Esme tried to bite back a smile, but it proved impossible. "I did. So, imagine my surprise when you show up with a dog that he found."

"That is quite the coincidence," Addy said. "How did you leave things? I mean, he's coming back."

"It was a one-night stand."

"But he's sending you letters. Why would he do that if he didn't want more?" Addy leaned forward and tapped the envelope. "He seems like a stand-up guy."

"He really is one of the good ones," Esme admitted. "But I don't have time for a relationship. And he has his own baggage."

Addy arched a brow. "So. Good sex and deep conversation. It seems to me the universe is telling you this man is worth getting to know."

"I don't know. Jillian still has a long road ahead of her and I'm barely holding it together between trying to get my asshole ex-husband to give me money and keep him out of Jillian's life and figure out how I'm going to keep this rental. Of course, my landlord might list anyway."

"I can give you some money if you need it," Addy said.

She hated taking handouts from anyone. "I know. I'm not that bad yet. But if all goes well, I'll be working full time in Jillian's school and not just tutoring. That should really help."

"Well, don't let things get too bad before calling." Addy patted her hand. "And go out on a date or two. Because if he knows about what's going on in your life and he's still writing to you? He's a keeper." Addy kissed Esme's cheek and skipped off to spend a few moments with Jillian and Jobe before she headed for home.

Esme held up the letter. It was hard not to feel all warm and fuzzy. It was nice when anyone thought enough about her to send a note. A text. Or call. After Jillian got sick, her friends all offered to be there for her, but most disappeared when the going got real tough. She understood how hard it was and people had lives, but a simple gesture often made her day.

She ripped open the envelope and spread out the paper.

Dear Esme,

I know this is pretty bold of me, but your note had your address on it and I just can't stop thinking about you. And it's not because I'm currently a mile under the surface with a bunch of ornery sailors. I can't close my eyes at night without seeing your smile or hearing your laugh. I know. Cheesy. I'm the king of cheesy.

Esme covered her mouth and stifled a laugh. Even in letter writing he was a bit of a dork.

I wish I could have said a proper goodbye, but I totally understand and your note meant a lot. I hope Jillian is doing well and has finished her treatments in the hospital and is now at home. I know this is all hard and I honestly wish I could be there for you. I know that sounds weird. But when I return, if you need anything at all, you can count on me. I mean that. If nothing else, please write me back and let me know how she's doing. I know I never met her, but I think of her too. Perhaps that's the residual effect of having, well, you know. I will be there for you. I promise.

Funny thing happened the day I left. I found a puppy under my porch. I named him Jobe, after my childhood dog. I'm hoping to find him when I return. The girl renting my place was going to try to find him a home and I left a note. I'm rambling. I'm not a very good letter writer. I kind of don't know what to say to you. I had always planned on putting myself out there, looking for someone special when I returned. I never expected to meet someone so incredible before my deployment. I mean, I spent three months in Newport doing training, looking for a place to rent short term, and I wasn't spending time going out.

And then there you were.

I just hope you'll give me a chance when I get back.

Anyway, feel free to write me. It takes a few weeks to get to me, so I could be halfway home by the time I get one, but still. I'd like it. If you want. No pressure.

Which I think is a passive-aggressive form of pressure. Ha ha. Me and my psychology degree.

Hope to hear from you.

Be well.

Sincerely,

Zayden

She folded the paper and carefully slid it back into the envelope.

"So?" Addy asked, standing over her with her hands on her hips. "What did he want?"

"He wants to see me when he gets back and he hopes I'll write to him."

"Are you going to?"

"Yes," Esme admitted. She'd be a cruel woman if she didn't. And she'd do so tonight, making sure it got in the mailbox tomorrow. Zayden deserved a response. She just wasn't sure what she would do when he returned.

Though he would be hard to refuse, she had a lot to consider, and a daughter who had a say in the matter.

6

Zayden snatched the letter he'd been hoping to receive for weeks and double-timed it back to the captain's quarters as if he were five years old and he'd just gotten back from trick-or-treating and he wanted to sort out his candy. His heart raced and he had sweaty palms. He bumped into his first officer.

"Sorry, sir," First Officer Riley Gorman said.

"At ease. And my fault, Riley."

"Looks like you finally got what you've been waiting for." Riley pointed.

"I sure did. Now if you'd get the hell out of my way, I'd like to go read it."

Riley laughed as he stepped out of the way.

Once in the privacy of his room, Zayden plopped himself on his bunk and ripped open the letter, dated four weeks ago. Not horrible considering they'd just made the turn two weeks ago to return to port. He should be in Norfolk by September 15 and once debriefing was finished, back in Newport, Rhode Island, on the twentieth.

His first stop? Esme's doorstep.

Dear Zayden,

It was such a pleasant surprise to hear from you. I'm glad you took the time to write to me, cheesy and all.

He smiled.

Thank you for asking about Jillian. Most people kind of slide over the subject. And as much as everyone says they will help out or be there, and they mean well, when it gets tough, they aren't around.

Jillian is doing great. She's home and the treatment seems to be working. They are even talking that she will be able to go back to school in September.

I don't know when you will get this. It looks like it took a month for your letter to get to me. At this rate you might get one letter back to me and by the time my next letter gets to you, you'll be stateside.

I do need to be honest with you and tell you that the idea of getting involved in any kind of relationship outside of friendship not only scares the shit out of me, but I'm just not sure it's the right thing for my daughter. I know this isn't what you want to hear and maybe I'm being a bitch for writing this to you, but I do like you and I feel as though I need to always be honest with you.

I just don't know. As you can tell, I'm waffling. What does your psychology degree tell you about this letter? I mean I'm talking out of both sides of my mouth. I feel like I'm sort of stringing you along and I don't want to do that. I hope this all makes sense to you because I think the one glass of wine I've had tonight has gone right to my head.

You know how well I handle my alcohol. Haha.

Please be safe out there.

Talk soon.

Esme

He tucked the letter into his nightstand, with the other letter. He lay flat on his back and stared at the ceiling. The last thing he wanted to do was push her into something she wasn't ready for, and taking care of a sick child, even one on the road to recovery was not only stressful, but it took up your entire world. For the last few weeks he constantly checked his motives for wanting to be with Esme, and every time he went through his checklist, they all came out as pure.

He genuinely cared for her.

So much so that he would back off if that's what she needed.

But he could also be a friend and based on that letter, she needed a few good ones.

A tap on his door pulled him from his thoughts. "Door's open."

"Sorry, sir," Riley said, snapping to attention.

"At ease."

"You've got comms coming in from Newport. It's a Lieutenant Colonel Karl Rector."

"I'll be right there." Zayden couldn't imagine why Karl would need to reach him, but a million things went through his mind and none of them were good. He put on his officer's coat and hat and made his way to the bridge. "Clear the bridge," he said. His staff did as instructed. He took over the comms, putting big old-fashioned earphones on. He adjusted the microphone. "Karl? Are you there?" Static filled his ears.

"I'm here."

"What's going on?"

"Some woman by the name Addy Waldman has been practically banging down the doors of any Navy personnel that will listen to her, asking to get ahold of you for the last eight days. How do you know this person?" Karl asked.

"She subleased my apartment. But she left like two months ago. What does she want?" He rubbed his forehead. He'd met the girl for like an hour. And would she go to this length over a dog? That didn't make sense, especially when the landlord said she'd packed up and moved.

"Something about her sister being in a car accident and needing you."

"I didn't know she had a sister. I have no idea what she's talking about."

"Maybe she's just a freak."

"Perhaps." Zayden rolled his neck. "What's the sister's name?"

"Esme Cole."

"Shit." He swallowed the lump in his throat. Cole must be Esme's married name. Made sense. And Addy could be short for Adeline. "I know Esme. How bad was the car accident and where is her daughter?"

"I don't know anything about a daughter, but I saw the accident on the news. It was bad. Real bad. I believe she's still in the hospital."

Tears burned his eyes. "Fuck. You've got to get me off this sub and in Newport yesterday. I don't care how you do it. I don't care if they fucking court martial me. Just make it happen."

"Who is this woman to you?"

"The one I'm not going to let get away. And I'll be damned if I'm going to make the same mistake twice." He stood. "I'm going to bring this submarine to the surface. I expect a transport helicopter ready."

"She's not your wife. She's not family. No one is—"

"Her daughter has leukemia."

"I see. But that doesn't change things," Karl said.

"I don't care what you say to make it happen. Just get me off this fucking submarine. Or I will jump."

"Don't do anything that drastic," Karl said. "Let me see what I can do."

"Make it happen." Zayden pulled the earphones from his head and called the crew back into the bridge. "We're going to surface and I'm going to be leaving the ship. Hardy will be in charge during my absence." He left the crew standing in the bridge with their jaws slacked open while he double-timed it back to his cabin to pack.

No way would he leave Esme to sit in a hospital bed alone.

Nor would he leave her daughter to worry by herself.

7

*Z*ayden nearly ran right into the double sliding glass doors to the main entrance at Newport Hospital. He adjusted his rucksack over his shoulder. He hadn't even stopped at his rental after landing at the base. He'd been traveling for twenty-four hours straight and he probably smelled like the back of the C-130 transport plane, which reminded him of a combination of sweaty socks and damp cloths. He made his way to the information desk and smiled at the young man. "Hi. I'm looking for a patient. Esme Cole."

"Okay. I can look her up for you." He tapped on his keyboard and stared at a computer screen. "She was just moved to a private room."

"So, she's no longer critical?" Zayden held his breath.

"No. Her condition is listed as stable."

"Thank God," he mumbled. "When was she moved?" He'd requested that private room and paid for it, something that he knew was going to piss her off, but he'd deal with it later. Her insurance would only pay for so much and he just wanted the best care for her, and this would also allow for her daughter to visit without having to worry about whoever was on the other side of the curtain in a double room. With her compromised immune system, they needed to be as safe as possible.

"Yesterday."

"And her room number?"

"Zayden?" a familiar voice rang out from somewhere behind him.

He turned. "Addy? Or should I say Adeline?"

"The only person who calls me that is Esme when she's pissed off." Addy stretched out her arm.

He took her hand and shook it.

"I can't believe you're here."

"I'm shocked you didn't get yourself arrested. My buddy Karl said you made quite a pest of yourself."

She nodded as a single tear rolled down her cheek. "I don't know much about what went on between you and my sister other than the few times we talked about you, her eyes became so vibrant and I haven't seen her like that since Jillian was born, and even then, that was tainted because her ex is such a douchebag."

Zayden laughed. "Why don't you tell me how you really feel?" He followed her down the corridor, passing a family with a few kids.

"I don't think that would be smart. You being a sailor, I'm sure you've heard it all, but I don't think anyone in this hospital wants to hear me cuss like a drunken fool."

He glanced toward the ceiling while they waited for the elevator. He blew out a puff of air. "I've been traveling for close to two days. I haven't had a chance to find out too much about what is going on. All I know is that she was T-boned and they had to cut her from the car."

"I'm so grateful Jillian wasn't with her. The entire passenger side of the car was crushed like an accordion." She swiped at her cheeks and sucked in a deep breath.

He could tell it was taking a lot of energy for her to keep it together and be strong for her family.

They stepped into the elevator and she hit the fifth floor.

"Both her lungs were punctured. A piece of metal went into her side and did some damage to one of her kidneys, but they were able to repair all that. However, she suffered brain trauma and they had to put her into a medically induced coma. She woke up about five days ago."

"And how is she?"

Addy cupped her face and burst out crying. "She seems to be fine."

He pulled her close and patted her back. "What do the doctors say?"

"The swelling in her brain is gone and she's going to be okay. They said she could be released in a few days." Addy took a step back and brushed her hair from her face. "I'm sorry."

"Don't be. It's been a long ten days for you. I just wish you could have gotten to me sooner."

"To be honest, I sort of can't believe you're here. Like I said, my sister hasn't told me much."

"Whatever she said, you felt the need to go out of your way to find me." The elevator doors opened. He followed her through hallways. The thick scent of antiseptic covered up his days of travel. "And thank you for that. I really appreciate it."

"She's going to kill me for telling you, but you're one of the first people she asked for when she woke up, only she was so drugged she was clueless."

"Now you're just trying to make me feel good

while playing matchmaker at the same time," he said with a slight laugh.

"Nope on the first point. And maybe just a little on the second." She held up her fingers, making the inch sign. "She really likes you."

"I more than like her," he admitted, standing in front of the door with Esme's name written on the whiteboard hanging on a tack. "Where is Jillian?"

"It's actually treatment day, so she's in the children's wing. I was just headed there when I ran into you. I was going to leave a message for you at the desk, in case you showed up asking for directions." She leaned in and kissed his cheek. "Thank you."

He sucked in a deep breath and pushed open the door. All the air in his lungs escaped as if someone sat on them, forcing it out in one big swoop. He tried to suck in another breath, but it fell short.

Setting his rucksack on the chair by the door, he inched closer to the bed.

Esme lay under a blanket with wires, IVs, and machines hooked up to her body. Her right arm had a cast on it and her left leg was elevated, also in a cast. Her pale face sported a few bruises. She moaned, licking her lips and tilting her head. "Addy?" she whispered.

"No. It's Zayden."

Her eyes blinked open. She shifted in the bed and groaned.

He rushed to her side, taking her good hand. "Don't move."

"I hate these drugs."

"But you need them," he said. "For the pain and other things."

She rolled her head to the side. Her eyelids fluttered. "True. But they give me crazy dreams."

"Oh yeah. Like what?"

"Like Zayden being at my bedside. As if he could leave the middle of the Pacific Ocean on his last month of his tour just to be with me."

He sat on the edge of the bed, leaned over, and kissed her temple. "Babe, I'm right here. Live. In the flesh. Holding your hand."

"Wouldn't that be nice. Then I could tell you how much I really wanted to see you when you got home. That the only thing I'm afraid of is letting anyone in because I don't want to get hurt again."

He pressed his lips gently on her cheek. "The last thing I ever want to do is hurt you," he whispered. "I moved heaven and earth to get here because I want to be with you. I want to see where this might go. I can't make you any promises but—"

She jerked her head back and groaned. "God,

that hurt." Palming his face, she pinched his cheek. "I'm not dreaming, am I?"

"Nope." He tried not to laugh, but it proved impossible. "Not only did I leave the middle of the Pacific to be here with you, I'm not going back so I can stay here and help take care of you."

"How is that possible? I'm not family. Won't you get like kicked out or something?"

He shook his head. "I'll have to do a few weekend things, but I'll start my new teaching job a little sooner than anticipated." He brushed some of her hair from her face, running his thumb under her cheek. "I know this is crazy. And way too soon. But I really care about you and I don't want to make the kinds of mistakes I made in the past."

"Don't you dare make me cry, Zayden."

His own eyes burned with hot tears. "I'll try not to, but you know me and cheesy lines."

She chuckled and moaned. "Or laugh. It hurts."

"Will it hurt too much if I kiss you?" he asked.

"I won't know until you do it."

He smiled, leaning closer. "We're crazy, you know that, right?"

"No. This is the sanest thing I've ever done."

He pressed his lips against her mouth softly and held them there for a long moment.

"Is that him?" a young girl asked.

He lifted his head, glancing over his shoulder.

"Are you Zayden?" the girl asked. She climbed up on the foot of the bed. She wore a pink dress with a white sweater and a pink sparkly baseball cap, and she carried a stuffed elephant.

He nodded. "You must be Jillian." He stood, still holding on to Esme's hand. "I've heard a lot about you."

"My auntie didn't think you'd be able to get here for a month or so." She tilted her head while hugging her toy.

"It took some doing, but I can't imagine being anywhere else," he said.

"My mommy said you helped her with a problem and you've become friends and that she wants you to come—"

"Jillian," Esme interrupted her daughter. "I don't think Zayden wants to hear about all of that."

"Oh. No. I do." He smiled wide. "Go ahead, Jillian. What did your mom say about me coming around?"

"You're impossible," Esme said under her breath.

He sat on the edge of the bed, running his thumb over the top of her hand.

Jillian shrugged. "Oh. She just wanted to know

if I was okay if maybe she went out on a date with you."

"And? How do you feel about that?" he asked.

"I guess it's okay," Jillian said, holding his gaze. "But you better not hurt my mommy, or I'll be very upset with you."

"I don't plan on it."

"Good," Jillian said. "Mommy, can I tell him?"

"Tell me what?" He glanced between mother and daughter.

"A surprise that I think will make you very happy," Esme said. Her eyelids drooped. She obviously struggled to stay awake. "I had hoped to tell you this differently, but this will work." She nodded to her daughter.

Jillian pulled out a small tablet from her elephant which was actually a bag, not a stuffed animal. She tapped on the screen and then handed it to Zayden. "Jobe has been looking over me for the last few months."

Chills dotted Zayden's skin. His eyes burned. He ran his finger over the video of Jobe and Jillian playing fetch in the backyard. "He's gotten so big."

"He's a good dog too," Esme added. "Imagine my surprise when I read that note."

"I bet," he said, wiping the tear that escaped his

eye. "I'm glad your sister brought him to you and that you kept him."

"You can have him back if you want," Jillian said.

Jesus. This family was going to make him cry. He sucked in a deep breath and reached for Jillian's hand. "No. He's your dog. I'm sure he'd rather watch over you than deal with me."

"You can come play with him anytime you want." Jillian leaned in and kissed his cheek.

He laughed. "Oh. I plan on being at your place. A lot."

But it was her mother he hoped to spend most of his time with. "We should let your mom get some sleep. How about you and me go get some food. I haven't had anything to eat in hours. Is that okay with you, Esme?"

"Actually, I was hoping you'd go shower. You smell," Esme said.

"Gee, thanks. But I was stuck on the back of a transport plane for hours."

"Mommy. Can he take me home? Jobe needs to be let out and fed."

"I'm sure he's got—"

"I'd love to." He leaned over and kissed Esme's temple. "I'm not going anywhere. I want to be in your life, if you'll have me," he whispered.

"Something tells me you're much like Jobe. All cute and cuddly and impossible to say no to." She smiled up at him. "Thank you for once again being my knight in shining armor."

"I didn't do anything."

"You showed up."

SIX MONTHS LATER...

EPILOGUE

SIX MONTHS LATER...

*E*sme sat on the back deck and watched as
Zayden and Jillian played fetch with Jobe.
Damn dog got more attention than she did. Of
course, it warmed her heart how much attention
Zayden gave Jillian, especially since her father had
pretty much disappeared and she planned on asking
him to terminate his parental rights.

If he wasn't going to pay or visit, he didn't
deserve to be a father.

Of course, there was the little—no huge—
surprise she had for her future husband.

Zayden jogged over to the deck and snagged his
beer. "That dog has way too much energy." He took
a few gulps. He pointed to her water. "Do you want
a glass of wine or something?"

"No. I'm good." He glanced at his watch. "It's

190

six. It's okay to start, lightweight."

She laughed, patting the wood step. "Have a seat, big fella."

"I always get nervous when you call me that."

"You should be very nervous," she said with a laugh. "I want to change our wedding date."

He nearly choked on his beer. "Why?" he asked with wide eyes. "I hope you don't want to push it out or postpone it altogether."

"Relax. I don't have cold feet." She ruffled his hair that he'd let grow a little too long. "You better get that cut before you get in trouble."

"I've got an appointment tomorrow. Now stop changing the subject and tell me what the heck is going on."

"Well, it's not like we're having some big wedding, so I thought maybe we could do it in two weeks."

He opened his mouth and only a grunt came out.

"You're so cute when you get flustered."

"I told you I'd marry you tomorrow. I don't need a wedding and when we got engaged you said you didn't need one either, but you wanted your sister here and you wanted Jillian involved. I'm good with that. So why the change of heart?"

"Well, my sister can be here whenever I tell her

to be and Jillian's happy." She reached out and palmed his cheek. "You're so good to her."

"She's easy to love."

"So are you." She pressed his lips against hers. "I'm pregnant."

He cocked his head back. "Say what?"

"You heard me."

"Well, I'll be damned." He raised his beer and chugged it. "I'm going to be a daddy, again." He smiled. "Because I love Jillian like she's my own."

"I know you do and she loves you back."

"Can we tell her now?"

She laughed. "You're like a kid in a candy store."

He wrapped his arms around her and pulled her close. "Finding Jobe was the second-best thing that ever happened to me."

"What's the first?"

"Stepping back into that bar and becoming your knight in shining armor."

"More like my Prince Charming," she said. There would never be another man for her, ever. She'd found everything she'd ever needed, right here in his arms.

The End.

SECOND CHANCE
CHRISTMAS

SECOND CHANCE CHRISTMAS

A Christmas Short Story

USA Today Bestseller
JEN TALTY

To the Crazy Florida Bunch. You really know who to kick a writer's muse into high gear!

1

"You've got to be kidding me." Angel Wahlberg fell back on her king-sized bed and stared at the ceiling. It had been a month since her husband had come over to collect the rest of his things. Four weeks since she thought having one last night of wild passion would be a good way to say goodbye. That lapse in judgment resulted in a positive pregnancy test.

A baby.

Damn. Darren had wanted a kid in the worst way, but she had refused him. In her mind, she had a valid reason for waiting. When he pressed, she gave him an ultimatum.

His response had been to pack a bag and leave.

In that time, they hadn't spoken much.

However, ever since their night together, he'd been calling her or texting her almost daily. Most of the time she ignored him or told him she was too busy, even for a cup of coffee.

Her cell vibrated the bed. She glanced at the screen and groaned.

Dorothy Wahlberg.

Wonderful. She tapped the accept button. "Hi, Dorothy."

"Hi, dear, how are you doing today?"

Angel flopped her arm over her eyes. She loved her mother-in-law, but Dorothy hadn't accepted that Angel and Darren had called it quits. Dorothy continued to do everything she could to bring Darren and Angel back together. "I'm well. How are you and Ed? Ready for the big Christmas blowout?" She shouldn't have accepted the job. There were other reputable event planners she could have recommended, including the one she'd used last year to help her with the party so she could kick back and relax. Not that she wanted to give business over to her competitors, but she didn't need to spend time with Darren and his family.

Not anymore.

"I am, knowing you're the one handling all the details. All I have to do is clean my house."

Angel wanted to laugh. The Wahlbergs were

loaded, and Dorothy had a cleaning crew in there twice a week. "I'll be over tomorrow with my team around ten."

"Yes. You mentioned that. Thank you," Dorothy said abruptly. "Is Darren there? I've been trying to reach him since yesterday."

"I'm sorry, Dorothy, but he's not here, and I don't expect him. I'm sure he's working undercover or something." There were times Angel wondered if Darren had a death wish, but mostly, he struggled to make deep connections with humans. He had always been aloof, but the last few months before they split up, he seemed more withdrawn than usual. Her therapist had said that could be normal with men in his career, especially if they had no outlet for their emotions. She'd urged him to speak with a counselor, and not only for them as a couple. Whatever demons he faced at work had spilled over into their personal lives, successfully ruining their marriage.

Dorothy sighed. "Why can't the two of you work things out? I don't understand. You were the perfect couple and so much in love."

"We grew apart," Angel said.

They had been far from perfect, but they had been good together for a long time.

Until they weren't.

"That's not a real answer," Dorothy said. "Something happened, and I wish the two of you would get it together and find a way to forgive each other."

"It's the only answer I have," Angel said. It had been Darren who called it quits. Not her. She'd been prepared to fight. Hell, she'd even set it up for them to go to counseling, springing it on him one afternoon. That hadn't worked out too well since he walked out of the shrink's office five minutes after he'd arrived and then disappeared for week by taking an undercover assignment.

She pinched the bridge of her nose. Yesterday, she thought after Christmas, she'd never have to see Darren's family again. Now with a baby on the way, she'd forever be an integral part of their lives.

And Darren's.

"Did Darren tell you that the blue house down the road from the Sagamore was for sale?"

Unfortunately, Angel had forgotten to turn off the Zillow alerts for the Bolton Landing area, and she'd seen it when it hit the market.

And just again the other day for a pending sale.

That had been her—no—their dream home. They'd fallen in love with it on the night he proposed while they sat on the edge of the dock at the Sagamore. On their honeymoon two years ago, they dubbed the blue house, *the Christmas House* because of all the pretty holiday lights and decorations. Angel had always been a sucker for Christmas and tended to overdo the holiday spirit, which drove Darren crazy. However, he loved the tasteful décor of the Christmas House and readily agreed that if the home ever went on the market, they needed to snatch it up and make it their own.

"He didn't tell me that," Angel said softly.

Ding. Dong.

"I've got to go. Someone's at the door. I'll see you tomorrow," Angel said quickly, needing to get Dorothy off the phone. Angel couldn't stand thinking about the house on the lake anymore. That was a dream of the past and had nothing to do with her future.

"If you hear from him, please tell him I need to speak with him," Dorothy said.

"Sure thing." Angel tossed her cell on the bed and padded across the room and down the hall, ignoring the framed wedding picture lying against the wall. Talk about a perfect day. Everyone thought they were crazy to have an outdoor wedding in December, but the Sagamore did them right with outdoor heaters. The sun had danced across the freshly fallen snow, making everything sparkle. It had been the most beautiful day ever. Angel glanced at her watch.

In less than a week, she'd be celebrating her two-year anniversary, alone.

She should have never gotten married on New Year's Eve. What a dumb mistake.

She tucked a stray strand of hair behind her ear before pulling open the front door. She gasped. "Darren? What are you doing here? And in uniform?" She let her gaze roam up and down his taut body. His dark police shirt hugged his biceps like a second skin. His chest puffed out proudly.

And hot damn, he had buzzed his hair and shaved the scruff off his face.

He looked like the man she'd fallen in love with. The man she remembered, not the person who cared more about his career than his wife.

"Why aren't you dressed?" he asked, tucking his cap under his armpit.

She lowered her gaze to her bare toes. "I'm not going out for a few hours," she said, holding the wood frame, hoping he didn't notice her trembling hands. "While I've got you standing there, your mother just called. She said she's been trying to reach you."

"Thanks." He palmed the back of his neck and rubbed. "Did you really forget what today is?"

"Oh shit." She remained in the doorway, not wanting to invite him into her space. It had taken a while for her to get used to living in their apartment alone. She had no desire to be reminded what it was like to have him at her side. It was bad enough she had to smell his manly aftershave. She flattened her hand across her firm belly. Soon enough, it would be swelling, and she'd have to tell him. "I told you I wasn't going to attend, much less attend with you."

"May I come in?" he asked.

She glanced over her shoulder. Not that he'd go into the bedroom, but she'd left the pregnancy test on the bed, and until she'd been seen by the doctor, this news would be kept a secret.

"I've got a lot of things to do today in preparation for your parents' party tomorrow. I don't have much time."

He took his cap and fiddled with the emblem on the front. His gaze lowered, and he shifted from side to side. "Bradly Johnson was the best man at our wedding. You need to be at his memorial service." Darren lifted his head. His eyes welled with tears. "Sally was your friend."

"I went to the funeral." She curled her fingers around Darren's massive forearm, pulling him inside. "I know he was your best friend, and I'm sorry, but I can't go."

"Are you still hung up on the fact he died during an undercover operation? Sally is the one without a husband, not you. This memorial means a lot to her, and you should be there."

A short gasp exploded from her gut. She covered her mouth. "I have lost my husband," Angel whispered. She clutched her chest. Her lungs burned with each breath. "You and I are not a couple, and I'm not going to a service where I'll be expected to play wife."

Darren fell onto the sofa and laughed. "I'm not asking you to play anything. You don't even have to talk to me there if you don't want, but Sally, and her family, would be upset if you didn't show."

"My days as a cop's wife are over." She folded her arm across her middle. Butterflies took flight in her belly.

"So, just like that, because he was killed while undercover, you refuse to attend a memorial," Darren said with a bitter tone. "Officers get killed all the time in the line of duty; why must you focus on the undercover part all the time?"

"Jesus, Darren. This is not the time to fight with me over semantics."

"Did you know he died in my arms? He took his last breath while begging me to tell his wife how much he loved her. Did you know I was the one who had to tell Sally her husband had been killed?"

"No. I didn't know that." She turned her gaze to the picture window. A part of her wanted to sit next to him and cradle his head in her lap. Darren might be a lot of things, but he was a man of compassion, and Bradly was like a brother. They had grown up together and joined the force at the same time. They were as thick as thieves, even when Bradly had called Darren on his bullshit. "I'm really sorry. I am. Bradly was a good man, but—"

"Fine. Don't come. I'll give Sally your best."

A wave of dizziness swirled around her mind. Nausea gripped her gut. She sat on the sofa with a crushing pain in her chest. The fact that Darren had been a cop had never been the problem. She knew his job was dangerous, and she accepted that.

What she struggled with was how he'd changed when he went undercover.

Shit. Without a doubt, she knew she should go. It was the right thing to do. "I would need a half hour to get ready."

"Thank you," he said softly. "I need to tell you something."

"Can't it wait?" She picked at her thumbnail. "If you want me to go with you, I need to go get dressed now."

"I've been trying to tell you this for a while now, but you won't spend any time with me."

"What is it?" she asked.

"I took a promotion a couple of weeks ago. No more undercover assignments for me anymore," he blurted out.

"What kind of promotion?" She balled her fists. Heat prickled her veins.

"You're looking at the new commanding officer in charge of homicide detectives." He lifted his palms toward the celling before dramatically dropping them in his lap. "I know, I passed on the job six months ago, but a lot has changed."

She bolted to her feet. "I begged you to take that promotion, and you couldn't do it, not even if it could save our marriage, and now you randomly decide it's time? You're an asshole."

"Seriously? You're going to go there when you're the one who closed the book on us. Hell, I've been trying to talk to you for the last month, and you won't give me the time of day."

She bolted to a standing position. "On no, don't you dare. I wanted to go to counseling. I wanted to do whatever it took to try to make us work, but you—"

"I wanted a family, and all you did was give me a list of mandatory changes I had to make before you'd even consider having a child. I never once asked you to change who you were, and yet you needed to change everything about me. I freaked out and behaved badly. A month ago, I came groveling at your feet. I thought we'd made some progress, but you tossed me out on my ass in the morning. Ever since then, you've been running. All I'm asking is for a second chance to show you that I'm—"

"I'm not doing this with you right now. I will go with you to the memorial because it's the right thing to do. But please, stay out of my way tomorrow. I'm not at your parents' party as your wife or even a member of the family. I'm the hired help. Simple as that." With a heavy heart, she inched toward the bedroom. "Maybe it's better if I take my own car."

"No. We need to go together. Can you do this one thing for me? Please?" He stood tall, puffing out his chest.

Angel shook her head. "I won't pretend that we are back together."

"I'm not asking you to. Sally has been asking for you, and I know she'd like you to be there."

Angel drew in a deep breath. "I haven't spoken to her in over a month." When marriages ended, so did friendships, and Sally hadn't returned her last call or text. Angel understood, and she didn't hold it against Sally, especially with all she'd had to deal with since the death of her husband.

Darren rested a tender hand on her shoulder. "She's going to need a friend."

"She's got plenty."

"She's pregnant."

2

---

*D*arren had done his best to avoid his wife for the first few months after their big blowout. He had hoped the separation would help him to get over her, but all it did was make him miserable.

Bradly had told him he'd been stupid as fuck to leave Angel. Deep down, Darren knew his best friend had been right.

Now Bradly was dead.

Darren was even more alone.

And he wasn't even close to winning back his wife.

He leaned against his unmarked vehicle and sipped a water that Sally had given him and stared at the main building of the local country club. Large puffy snowflakes floated from the sky as if in slow motion. Over the years, Darren had seen a lot of death in his career, but he'd never had anyone die in his arms, making him promise he'd correct the biggest mistake of his life.

The front door swung open, and Angel stepped onto the sidewalk adjusting her sunglasses over her eyes. She pulled her parka tight and flipped the furry hood over her head. Her long reddish hair bounced over her shoulders. She kept her gaze to the ground as she made her way toward him. He didn't think he could have handled the memorial and saying a few words without Angel at his side.

Actually, he wondered how he'd managed to get up every day without her, but every time they were alone, and he opened his mouth, he spewed resentment in her direction. Even when he was trying to be remorseful, his stupid pride got in the way.

"Thank you," he whispered as she approached. "You being here meant a lot to me."

She raised her hand and tucked a finger under the rim of her glasses. "You're welcome." She snagged the water bottle from his hand and chugged. A gust of wind sent a cold shiver across his exposed skin.

"We need to talk about some things," he said,

wanting to clear the air. "Will you have dinner with me tonight?"

"I can't. I've got too much stuff to do for your parents, but you're right. We do need to have a conversation. I was going to wait until after Christmas, but I think I need to do this now." She dug her hand into her oversized bag. For as long as he'd known her, she had a thing for bags. She had to have at least one hundred. She couldn't walk into a store that carried purses without buying one. It drove him crazy.

"You've got the divorce papers already?" he asked.

"Oh, my God. You think I'd do that now? Here?" She hugged her purse with what looked like a thick sharpie of something in her hand. "You can be a real jerk sometimes, you know that?"

"You've mentioned that before." He lifted her chin with his thumb and forefinger. Her cheeks had turned a rosy red from the winter chill in the air. "I'm sorry. I'm barely holding it together, but now that I'm the commanding officer, I have to be everyone's rock, and I'm taking all my frustrations and pain out on you."

"With you, I'm an easy mark," she mumbled. "I have something big to tell you. I wanted to find the right moment, but if I waited for that, I'd be showing before I got the courage."

"Showing what? Are you moving?" He dropped his hand and narrowed his eyes. "Are you seeing someone?"

"No," she said firmly. "I'm pregnant." She poked him with the pen.

Or was it a stick? He couldn't be sure. He snagged the object and stared at the big blue plus sign at the end. "You're what-nant?" He coughed out. His thighs grew weak, and he had to steady himself against his car. The frozen metal tingled his fingertips. "Are you sure?"

"It hasn't been confirmed with the doctor yet. I have an appointment the day after Christmas."

"Who's the father?" He flicked his wrist as if it would make the plus sign turn negative.

"I should slap you for that remark," she said behind gritted teeth.

"It's a legit question. We haven't been together…oh, I almost forgot about that." His heart dropped to his gut, pounding erratically. Memories flooded his brain, taking over his thoughts, clouding his judgment.

"Wonderful. I'm forgettable. Well, that forgettable night produced an unforgettable little person."

"You are far from unmemorable," he managed to croak out while he shoved his foot factiously down his throat. "Let's sit in the car." He scratched the side of his face as he unlocked the passenger seat, helping her inside.

A baby.

His pulse raged through his body like a burning wildfire. His life with Angel flashed in front of his mind. A montage of the happiest moments swirled around like a kaleidoscope. His chest tightened, and he couldn't fill his lungs with enough air. He raced around the front before slipping behind the steering wheel. "Ironic, isn't it? I took the job that you say could have saved our marriage, and you're carrying the one thing I wanted more than anything."

"If you wanted it, you would have fought for us, but you bailed." She flipped the hood of her parka down and ran her fingers through her thick hair, fluffing it. God, he could watch her play with her hair all day long and be utterly satisfied.

"I'm not the only one that ruined our relationship. Besides, not once did you ever try to stop me." He rubbed his temples. Death. Life. Divorce. He'd managed to turn his life into a shitshow. "You let me go."

"We could go on with this same old argument all day and continue to hurt each other, or we can figure out how to get along. That is unless you don't want anything to do with our…crap. I'm not going to say that."

"Good, because that would have been about the lowest blow ever." He reached out, taking her hand in his, fanning his thumb over her silky soft skin. "This is quite the surprise," he said, lacing his fingers through hers. He thumbed the diamond on her engagement ring. "You haven't taken off your rings."

"It feels weird when I do."

He held up his hand and wiggled his finger. "I came out of my last undercover op, and the first thing I did was put this bad boy on. Old habits die hard."

She laughed. "We've barely been married two years. How can you call that an old habit?"

"Ever since we got married, I feel naked without it. I always hated that I couldn't take it with me when I was on an op, even if it was just stuffed in my pocket somewhere."

"That would have been dangerous," she said softly.

He leaned across the front seat, palmed her cheek, and pressed his mouth against hers. It was a brief, but powerful moment. He missed her kissable lips and loving arms. For a long time, they had the kind of romance movies were made about, until he brought up wanting to start a family. He didn't see the point in waiting. They were in their early thirties, and neither of them were getting any younger.

But instead of having a rational conversation about it, she handed him a list of things he had to do before she'd even consider it, and he, in turn, had acted like an immature kid who couldn't handle the truth. "A baby, huh?" He raised her hand to his lips. "How are you feeling?"

"Fine. I literally had just taken the test right before you showed up. I don't feel any different, yet." She glanced at him, lifting her glasses to the top of her head. Her blue eyes sparkled like a rainbow in the sun. "Were you ever going to tell me about the promotion?"

"I've been trying to, but you haven't made it easy. My latest plan had been to tell you at my parents' party," he admitted. "I felt like I needed to do it in person."

"I have to say it hurts that you took that position after I practically begged you to get out of undercover work."

"You didn't beg me. You told me to get a desk job or quit or…" He shook his head. "Arguing about the past isn't going to help us deal with the future." He ran a hand down his face, his thumb and forefinger coming together on his chin. "Please don't get mad, but you are planning on keeping it, right?"

"Of course, I am. And I want you to be a part of his or her life. This is your kid, and I know how much family means to you."

"Family," he whispered. "I always envisioned living with my wife and kid. Maybe we should talk about that. Maybe we should put the brakes on our divorce."

"I don't know. We both threw in the towel pretty quickly when things got tough. Staying married because I'm having a baby doesn't seem like the answer. But we have to be able to co-parent together."

"What about counseling? You wanted that months ago."

"You're willing to speak to a therapist?" Her voice rose three octaves.

Swallowing his pride, he nodded. "I've been seeing one at work."

"Wow. I'm shocked." She shifted in the seat. "I think it would be good for us so we can navigate co-parenting together."

"What if I don't want to co-parent? What if I want us to get back together?"

"I'm sorry, Darren. But that's never going to happen. I'm finally at a place where I'm comfortable in my own skin. Besides, we're no good together. We'll be better parents if we do it from separate addresses." She patted his thigh. "Can you take me home now? I've got a lot of stuff to do."

"Sure thing." He let out an angry puff of air. Punching the gas, he jerked out into the street. She hadn't even given him or their marriage a second thought. Well, he was going to have to change her mind, and he'd start with an early Christmas present.

He wasn't about to let her push his well-laid plan aside.

*a*ngel did her best to act more like the hired help than one of the family. Thankfully, there were over a hundred guests, making it easier for her to blend in.

Except with Darren.

Every time she entered a room, he seemed to be two steps behind her, always trying to give her a hand or engage her in intelligent conversation.

If that wasn't weird enough, he would stand next to her with his hand on the small of her back, as if they were still a couple.

"Hey, you," he said as he sauntered into the kitchen. "My folks said you were packing things up, so I thought I'd come give you hand."

"Thanks, but I have a staff for that." She pointed toward the door. "They are loading the van as we—what the hell? Where did my van go?"

Darren chuckled.

"Why is that funny?"

"I tipped them and told them they could go," he said with a stupid grin. "Without you."

Her cheeks burned. "Why on earth would you do that?"

"Because I have a surprise for you."

When they'd first been married, she loved the way he would lavish her with gifts and often surprise her with little overnight trips. "I don't have time for this. I need to get home."

"Why? Do you have plans tonight? Tomorrow?"

She opened her mouth to spew lies, but all that escaped her lips was a god-awful gasp and a cough. She cleared her throat. "Not the point," she said sternly. "Just because I'm…I'm, you know," she said softly, glancing over her shoulders. "You didn't tell anyone, did you?"

"No. You asked me not to, and I agree that waiting until after the doctor's appointment before making an official announcement is what's best, especially because we need to talk about how we're going to do this and—"

She hushed him by pressing her finger against his full lips. "We have time for that. Right now, I'm dead tired, and I just want to climb in my own bed and go to sleep."

He planted his hands on his hips and crinkled his forehead. Whenever he furrowed his brow, she could expect terse words. "Humor me and come with me. If you don't want to stay where I'm taking you, then I'll bring you straight home."

She poked the center of his chest. "I know you, and you don't like to take no for an answer."

"You're right, I don't, and all I'm asking is that you come with me for at least the next hour. After that," he shrugged, "I promise I will do whatever it is you want me to."

She let out a long breath. An hour wouldn't kill her. She nodded.

"Great." He snagged her coat from the rack by the back door and draped it over her shoulders. "My Jeep is running." He looped his arm around her shoulders.

"This better be good," she mumbled as he opened the back door.

The cold smacked her face, making the skin across her lips tight. The white, nearly full moon hung low in the winter New York sky. She took his hand and hopped up into the passenger seat. "Do I get a hint?" she asked, feeling the same excitement that he used to create tickle her skin from the tip of her toes to her fingernails. It was like she'd been transported back to her childhood, and she'd been given the key to the biggest candy shop known to man.

"You'll figure it out soon enough."

She glanced out the window, watching the puffy snowflakes float like angels from the sky. Country music played softly through the Jeep's speakers. Darren tapped his fingers against his thick thighs as he eased into traffic. She rested her head against the glass and closed her eyes. The next ten minutes were driven in silence. She palmed her stomach, imagining what it might feel like to have a tiny little foot pressing against her belly. "It was never that I didn't want to have a child with you."

"I know," he said, keeping his gaze on the road ahead.

"If that's the case, why did you leave?"

"Because I'm a big stubborn fool."

She wouldn't argue that point.

"I thought you'd come after me, and when you didn't, I allowed my pride to get in the way, and ever since then, I've been doing all the things you wanted in order to win you back."

"Kind of hard to win me over when you don't tell me anything."

"Well, you haven't made speaking to you all that

easy. For the last month, you've essentially blocked all my calls. No matter how hard I've tried to communicate with you, all you've done is shut me down. I wanted you to see a changed man, and I wanted you to know that I was committed. I had every intention of doing that a few weeks ago, but you wouldn't take my calls or see me. So, I devised a plan to sweep you off your feet after my parents' party."

She dropped her head back and exhaled. "Don't do this, Darren."

"Do what?"

"Lie to me about some big master scheme to win me over when you only created it after you found out I was pregnant. Having a baby isn't a reason to stay in a bad marriage."

"I know I screwed up, and for the last few months, I made things impossible, but I can prove I had this night planned for weeks." He turned onto Route Nine, passing the Christmas House. A sale pending sigh swung in the breeze. "Look at that. They have Santa and his sleigh on the roof."

"I used to think things like were tacky, but they always manage to make their house look festive and homey." She stared at the Christmas lights, focusing on how the colors danced across the thin layer of ice. She remembered waking up the morning after he proposed and sitting by the water with a cup of coffee, her new engagement ring capturing the sunrays and sparkling like the Fourth of July. The blue and white house with a matching boathouse called to her from down the road. She and Darren fantasized about their future in that very home with a couple of kids, a dog, and a boat. They had bright plans for their life together, until Darren refused to give up his undercover work.

"I wonder if they would sell their outdoor decorations. Would you like that?"

She laughed. "If I was living there, sure."

"Did you go to the open house?"

She shook her head. "Why the hell would I torture myself like that?"

"Yeah. Well, it's even prettier inside than we ever imagined and the kitchen, oh, my God, you'll love it." He rolled to a stop in the parking lot of the Sagamore.

"Why are we here?" she asked. "I'm not in the mood to relive our romance. It was good while it lasted, but it's over."

"We're not over," he said as he pulled his cell out of his back pocket and tapped the screen. "I made this reservation two weeks ago." He held his phone up.

With a shaky hand, she took his cell and read

the date. Her eyes blurred. "You could have booked this for another wom—"

"There has never been another woman since you walked into my life," Darren said, taking her hand. "And there never will be. I have no excuse for being an asshole. I can only tell you that going undercover is addictive and giving up that rush, well, I thought I'd go crazy if I couldn't get that high from my work. But I was wrong. Devastatingly wrong." He leaned over and brushed his lips against her cheek. "I got us the same room we've always had." He flashed the plastic key. "I checked us in this morning."

"That's very presumptuous of you," she said as a tinge of anticipation crawled up her spine. He could be so romantic and attentive when he wanted to be, and God help her, she missed that.

Missed him.

"There are more surprises upstairs."

"I can't stay here tonight with you."

He let out a long breath. "Will you at least let me give you your Christmas gift? It's upstairs."

"As long as you promise you'll bring me home right after."

"If that's what you want, I will do exactly that." Sadness laced his words, but she refused to be the one responsible for his emotions.

He made his bed, now he had to sleep in it.

She slipped from the vehicle and let him lead her into the hotel. They made their way to room number eighty-six. A lifetime of memories bombarded her mind. Flashes of him getting on one knee down by the waterfront in a private moment when no one was looking. It had been the kind of proposal women dreamed about. He'd planned out every detail from the roses, to the location, to the spectacular private dinner cruise.

He'd made it impossible for her to say no.

Darren pushed open the hotel room door.

She stood in the threshold, holding her breath. Tears burned her eyes as she stared at the roses sitting on the bed, just as they had the night he proposed and on their wedding night. Everything in the room was identical, right down to the envelope on the table by the door with her name written on it.

"Do you remember what I wrote to you the day we got engaged?"

She nodded. "You know I do. I had that note and the one you gave me on our wedding night framed."

"I still think that's weird." He lifted the envelope and handed it to her. "I'm going to go to the bar while you read this. If you still want to go home, I'll

227

take you. No pressure." He didn't wait for her answer as he left her standing alone in the one space that forever would belong to the memory of them.

The paper burned her fingertips, and she fumbled to get it open. Taking a seat on the bed, she spread out the note. Attached to the bottom with some clear tape was a key. She ripped the tape off and fingered the metal object while she found the courage to read.

Dear Angel,

My Angel. I've made so many mistakes, and I don't blame you if you don't want to give us a second chance. I was a jerk and treated you about as badly as a husband could, and I will forever try to make that up to you, no matter what happens. You deserve better than that.

I was so angry and hurt that I couldn't even see your side. All I heard was that you didn't want to have a baby with me. I made myself believe you didn't think I was good enough. I know that's not true. I also know you never wanted to change me. You never wanted me to quit being a cop. I know that all you wanted was me to be present.

I'm present.

I'm here.

I will love you always, no matter what. You are in my blood. You are under my skin.

You, my Angel, are my world.

This key is in part a symbol of my love. It's the key to the future we discussed the morning after you accepted my proposal. The Christmas house on the point can be ours. I hope this holiday you will take a second chance and allow me to be the husband you deserve.

I love you,

Darren, the big fool.

She swiped at her cheeks and swallowed a guttural sob. Gripping the key, she raced from the room. Her heart thumped in her throat. She pressed the elevator button five times before the stupid doors finally opened. It took forever to make it to the bottom floor where she nearly knocked over some old couple.

Once inside the bar, she scanned the room.

He had perched himself at the bar with his back to the lobby.

"Darren," she called.

He turned. "That was fast, and I don't know if that's good or bad."

"Did you do it? Did you really do it?" She held up the key.

"You should see the fireplace in the living room. It's more spectacular than we imagined."

"You really bought it?"

"It's ours if we want it." He pulled a folded paper from the inside of his sport coat. "I made the offer a couple of weeks ago. All of this was done long before I found out about the baby. I love you, Angel, and I'm lost without you. Please. I'm begging, take me back. Give our family a second chance Christmas."

"That's what we'll name the house. And the boat. You are going to buy us a boat, right?"

"Right after I get the black lab," he said with a bright smile and outstretched arms. "Come here."

She didn't hesitate and flung herself at him, crash-landing her lips on his. "I love you," she whispered. "Shall we go back up to our room and seal this deal?"

Thank you for taking the time to read *Second Chance Christmas*. I hope you enjoyed!

ABOUT THE AUTHOR

Jen Talty is the *USA Today* Bestselling Author of Contemporary Romance, Romantic Suspense, and Paranormal Romance. In the fall of 2020, her short story was selected and featured in a 1001 Dark Nights Anthology. She is currently contracted to write in the *With Me in Seattle* series by Kristen Proby with Lady Boss Press, as well as Susan Stoker's *Special Forces: Operation Alpha* and Elle James's *Brotherhood Protectors.*

Regardless of the genre, her goal is to take you on a ride that will leave you floating under the sun with warmth in your heart. She writes stories about broken heroes and heroines who aren't necessarily looking for romance, but in the end, they find the kind of love books are written about :).

She first started writing while carting her kids to one hockey rink after the other, averaging 170 games per year between 3 kids in 2 countries and 5 states. Her first book, IN TWO WEEKS was originally published in 2007. In 2010 she helped form a publishing company (Cool Gus Publishing) with *NY Times* Bestselling Author Bob Mayer where she ran the technical side of the business through 2016.

Jen is currently enjoying the next phase of her life…the empty nester! She and her husband reside in Jupiter, Florida.

Grab a glass of vino, kick back, relax, and let the romance roll in…

Sign up for my Newsletter (https://dl.bookfunnel.com/82gm8b9k4y) where I often give away free books before publication.

Join my private Facebook group (https://www.facebook.com/groups/191706547909047/) where I post exclusive excerpts and discuss all things murder and love!

And on Bookbub: bookbub.com/authors/jen-talty

facebook.com/AuthorJenTalty

instagram.com/jen_talty

bookbub.com/authors/jen-talty

amazon.com/author/jentalty

pinterest.com/jentalty

JOHNNIE WALKER

GEORGIA MOON

JACK DANIELS

JIM BEAM

WHISKEY SOUR

WHISKEY COBBLER

WHISKEY SMASH

Search and Rescue

PROTECTING AINSLEY

PROTECTING CLOVER

PROTECTING OLYMPIA

PROTECTING FREEDOM

PROTECTING PRINCESS

NY STATE TROOPER SERIES

In Two Weeks

Dark Water

Deadly Secrets

Murder in paradise Bay

To Protect His own

Deadly Seduction

When A Stranger Calls

His Deadly Past

The Corkscrew Killer

Brand New Novella for the First Responders series

A spin off from the NY State Troopers series

PLAYING WITH FIRE

PRIVATE CONVERSATION

THE RIGHT GROOM

AFTER THE FIRE

CAUGHT IN THE FLAMES

The Men of Thief Lake

REKINDLED

DESTINY'S DREAM

Federal Investigators

JANE DOE'S RETURN

THE BUTTERFLY MURDERS

The Aegis Network

THE LIGHTHOUSE

HER LAST HOPE

THE LAST FLIGHT

ROUGH AROUND THE EDGES

ROUGH RIDE

ROUGH EDGE

ROUGH BEAUTY

The Brotherhood Protectors

The Saving Series

SAVING LOVE

SAVING MAGNOLIA

SAVING LEATHER

Hot Hunks

Cove's Blind Date Blows Up

My Everyday Hero – Ledger

Tempting Tavor

Holiday Romances

A CHRISTMAS GETAWAY

ALASKAN CHRISTMAS

WHISPERS

CHRISTMAS IN THE SAND

CHRISTMAS IN JULY

Heroes & Heroines on the Field

TAKING A RISK

TEE TIME

The Twilight Crossing Series

THE BLIND DATE

SPRING FLING

SUMMER'S GONE

WINTER WEDDING

Witches and Werewolves

LADY SASS

ALL THAT SASS